Here's Lily

Other Books Available in The Lily Series

Fiction

Lily Robbins, MD (Medical Dabbler)—coming soon!

Nonfiction

The Beauty Book

The Body Book—coming soon!

Here's Lily

Nancy Rue

NELSON

A Division of Thomas Nelson Publishers

NASHVILLE   DALLAS   MEXICO CITY   RIO DE JANEIRO

Here's Lily!
© 2012 Nancy Rue

Published in association with the literary agency of Alive Communications, Inc., 7680 Goddard Street, Suite 200, Colorado Springs, CO 80920. www.alivecommunications.com

Published in Nashville, Tennessee, by Tommy Nelson. Tommy Nelson is a registered trademark of Thomas Nelson, Inc.

Tommy Nelson® titles may be purchased in bulk for educational, business, fund-raising, or sales promotional use. For information, please e-mail SpecialMarkets@ThomasNelson.com.

Library of Congress Cataloging-in-Publication Data

Rue, Nancy N.
  Here's Lily! / Nancy Rue.
    p. cm. -- (Lily series)
  Summary: "Grow with the spirited, sometimes awkward, but always charming Lily as she learns what real beauty is. In this fun, entertaining story, readers meet awkward sixth grader Lily Robbins who, after receiving a compliment about her looks from a woman in the modeling business, becomes obsessed with her appearance and with becoming a model. As she sets her sights on winning the model search fashion show, she exchanges her rock and feather collection for lip gloss, fashion magazines, and a private "club" with her closest friends. But when the unthinkable happens the night before the fashion show, Lily learns a valuable lesson about real beauty. This best-selling, biblically based fiction series for girls--with a fresh new look and updated content--addresses social issues and coming-of-age topics, all with the spunk and humor of Lily Robbins as she fumbles her way through unfamiliar territory. As readers come to love Lily and her stories, they'll also benefit from the companion nonfiction books that will help them through their own growing pains"-- Provided by publisher.
  ISBN 978-1-4003-1949-7 (pbk.)
  [1. Beauty, Personal--Fiction. 2. Models (Persons)--Fiction. 3. Self-confidence--Fiction. 4. Christian life--Fiction.] I. Title. II. Title: Here is Lily!
  PZ7.R88515He 2012
  [Fic]--dc23   2011053209

Printed in the United States of America

12 13 14 15 16 QG 6 5 4 3 2 1

One

*L*eo, don't let it touch you, man! It'll burn your skin off!"
Shad Shifferdecker grabbed his friend's arm and yanked him away from the water fountain just as Lily Robbins leaned over to take a drink. Leo barely missed being brushed by Lily's long flaming red hair.

Lily straightened up and drove her vivid blue eyes into Shad.

"I need for you to quit making fun of my hair," she said through gritted teeth. She always gritted her teeth when she talked to Shad Shifferdecker.

"Why can't you ever just say 'shut up'?" Shad said. "Why do you always have to sound like a counselor or something?"

Lily didn't know what a counselor sounded like. She'd never been to one. If Shad had, it hadn't helped much as far as she was concerned. He was still rude.

"I'm just being polite," Lily said.

Leo blinked his enormous gray eyes at Shad. "Shad, can you say 'polite'?"

"Shut up," Shad said and gave Leo a shove that landed him up against Daniel Tibbetts, his other partner in seeing how hateful a sixth-grade boy can be to a sixth-grade girl.

1

Just then Ms. Gooch appeared at the head of the line, next to the water fountain, and held up her right hand. Hands shot up along the line as mouths closed and most everybody craned their necks to see her. Ms. Gooch was almost shorter than Lily.

"All right, people." Lily was glad she didn't call them "boys and girls" the way the librarian did. "We're going to split up now. Boys will come with me. Girls will go into the library."

"How come?" Shad blurted out as usual.

"The girls are going to a grooming workshop," Ms. Gooch said. She raised an eyebrow. Ms. Gooch could say more with one black eyebrow than most people could with a whole sentence. "Did you want to go with the girls and learn how to fix your hair and have great skin, Shad? I'm sure they'd love to have you."

"No, we would not," Lily wanted to say. But she never blurted it out. She just turned to Reni and rolled her eyes.

Reni rolled hers back. That was the thing about best friends, Lily had decided a while back. You could have entire conversations with each other just by rolling your eyes or saying one key word that sent you both into giggle spasms.

"No way!" Shad said. "I don't want to look like no girl!"

"Any girl," Ms. Gooch said. "All right, ladies, go on to the library. Come back with beauty secrets!"

Lily took off on Reni's heels in the direction of the library. Behind her, she heard Shad say, just loud enough for her to hear, "That grooming lady better be pretty good if she's gonna do anything with Lily!"

"Yeah, dude!" Leo said.

Daniel just snorted.

"Ignore them," Reni whispered to Lily as they pushed through the double doors to the inside of the school. "My mama says when boys say things like that, it means they like you."

"Gross me out and make me icky," Lily said, wrinkling her nose.

Besides, that was easy for Reni to say. Lily thought Reni was about the cutest girl in the whole sixth grade. She was black (Ms. Gooch said they were supposed to call her "African American," but Reni said that took too long to say), and her skin was the smooth, rich color of Lily's dad's coffee when he put a couple drops of milk in it. *Mine's more like the milk without the coffee!* Lily thought.

And even though Reni's hair was a hundred times curlier than Lily's naturally frizzy mass of auburn, it was always in little pigtails or braids or something. Reni's hair was under control anyway. Lily's brother Art said Lily's hair always looked like it was enough for thirty-seven people the way it stuck out all over her head.

But most important of all, Reni was as petite and dainty as a toy poodle, not tall and leggy like a giraffe. At least that was the way Lily thought of herself. Even now, as they walked into the library, Lily tripped on the wipe-your-feet mat and plowed into a rolling rack of books. She rolled with it right into Mrs. Blain, the librarian, who said, "Boys and girls, please be careful where you're walking."

It's just girls, Lily wanted to say to her. *And I'm so glad.* Shad Shifferdecker definitely would have had something to say about *that* little move.

Reni steered her to a seat in the front row of the

half circles that had been formed in the middle of the library. The chairs faced a woman who was busily taking brushes and combs and tubes of things out of a classy-looking leather bag and setting them on a table. Lily watched her for a minute.

The lady wore her blond hair short and obviously styled with product, the way all the women did on TV. Her nails were shiny and had perfect white tips. They clacked lightly against the table when she set things down on it. Lily could smell her from the front row. She smelled expensive, like a department store cosmetics counter.

Lily thought about how her mother grabbed lipstick while they were shopping for groceries at the Acme and then only put it on when Dad dragged her to some university faculty party. As for having her nails done—high school P.E. teachers didn't *have* fingernails.

Lily's mind and eyes wandered off to the bookshelves. *I'd much rather be finding a book on Indian headdresses*, she thought as she looked wistfully at the plastic book covers shining under the lights. Her class was doing reports on Native Americans, and she had a whole bunch of feathers at home that she'd collected from their family's camping trips. *Wouldn't it be cool to make an actual headdress . . .*

"May I have your attention please, ladies?"

Reluctantly Lily looked at the lady with the white-tipped nails and wondered vaguely just how she got them that way. She was facing them now, and Lily saw that she had on lipstick that matched her sweater, put on without a smudge, and gold hoop earrings that brushed against her cheek. Something about her made Lily tuck her own well-bitten nails under her thighs and wish she'd looked in the mirror before she came in here to make sure she didn't have playground dirt smeared across her forehead.

Nah, she thought. *If I did, Shad Shifferdecker would've said something about it.*

Besides, the lady had a sparkle in her eyes that made it seem like she could totally take on Shad Shifferdecker. Lily liked that.

"I'm Kathleen Winfrey," the lady was saying, "and I'm from the Rutledge Modeling Agency here in Burlington."

An excited murmur went through the girls, followed by a bunch of hands shooting up.

"Well!"

Kathleen Winfrey smiled, revealing a row of very white, perfect teeth. Lily sucked in her full lips and hoped her mouth didn't look quite so big.

"Questions already?" Kathleen said. "I've barely started. How about you?"

She pointed to Marcie McCleary, who was waving her arm so hard that Lily knew all her rings were going to go flying across the library any second.

"You're from a modeling agency?" Marcie asked breathlessly. "Do you, like, hire models?"

"We hire them, and we train them," Kathleen said.

"Could we be models?" somebody else said.

"Is that why you're here—to pick models?"

"Do they do, like, commercials or just fashion shows and stuff?"

"I was at this fashion show at the mall, and this lady came up to my mother and said I could be a model like the ones they had there, and . . ."

"Ladies!" Kathleen laughed in a light, airy kind of

way that made Lily vow never to giggle like a hyena again. "Why don't I tell you why I *am* here and that will probably answer *all* your questions at once. I've come to Cedar Hills Middle School today to talk to you about taking good care of your hair and your skin and your nails, not to hire models."

The whole library seemed to give a disappointed sigh. Except Lily. It had never occurred to her to be a model in the first place, so what was there to be bummed out about? As for learning how to take good care of her hair and her skin and . . .

Lily pulled out her hands and scowled at the nails bitten down to the quicks. *I need all the help I can get*, she thought. That evil Shad Shifferdecker was probably right: this lady *better* be pretty good.

"Not everyone is model material," Kathleen went on. "Just as not everyone is doctor material or astronaut material—"

"Or boy material." That came from Ashley Adamson, *the* most boy-crazy girl in the *entire* school. Lily turned to Reni to roll her eyes just in time to see Ashley pointing right at her and whispering to Chelsea, her fellow boy-chaser. Lily could feel her face stinging as if Ashley had hauled off and slapped her.

"But every woman can be beautiful," Kathleen said. "And since you are all on the edge of young womanhood right now, I'd like to show you some ways that you can discover your own beauty."

This time Lily looked straight ahead so she couldn't see what Ashley was doing. It was enough that she heard Ashley sniff, as if she'd discovered her beauty long ago and could show *Kathleen* a thing or two.

"Now," Kathleen said, "I'm going to take you through some basics in skin care, and hair care, and nail care. But instead of just telling you, I'd like to show you. I'm going to pick someone."

She took a step forward, and hands sprang up and waved like seaweed. Marcie held on to her arm with the other hand as if she were afraid it would fall off, and Ashley's face went absolutely purple as she strained for Kathleen to see her. Even Reni raised her hand tentatively, although she looked at Lily as if to say, *She'll never pick me, so why am I bothering?*

Lily seemed to be the only one who wasn't begging Kathleen to look at her. If she did, she knew she'd have Ashley and Chelsea and some of the others hooting and pointing and whispering. *Lily? Her? Too-tall Lily? With too much red hair? Too big a mouth and too-thick lips? What are you thinking?!?*

Instead, Lily reached over, grabbed Reni's arm, and held it up even higher. It was at exactly that moment that Kathleen's eyes stopped scanning the desperate little crowd and rested on her.

"Ah . . . you," she said.

"Yay!" Lily squeezed Reni's hand. "She picked you, Reni!"

But Kathleen shook her head and smiled. "No, honey," she said to Lily. "I picked *you*."

Two

M e?" Lily's jaw dropped. The disappointed groans behind her were a sure sign nobody else believed it either. But Kathleen nodded and held out her hand. "Come on up. What's your name?"

"Lilianna," Lily said as she stood up stiff as a pole. "Lilianna Robbins, only everybody calls me Lily. It's easier."

"Great name!" Kathleen said. "All right, Lily, if you'll just sit down in the chair here. There we go."

She kept talking in her light-as-air way as Lily sank into the chair and once again tucked her hands under her thighs.

I sure hope she doesn't have time to get to fingernail care, Lily thought, *or this is going to be way embarrassing.*

She could already feel her face getting hot, and she knew there were probably red blotches all over it. Shad Shifferdecker had once said she looked like she had a disease when that happened.

"Now, Lily," Kathleen said, "would you mind if I pushed some of this gorgeous hair of yours away from your face so we can concentrate on skin first?"

Lily heard a couple of the girls snicker. She darted her eyes over to Reni. Her best friend was leaning forward in her chair, nodding fiercely at Lily. She was concentrating so hard, her dimples looked like poke holes.

"Sure," Lily agreed. "But you might have trouble getting a brush through it. My hair's kind of thick."

"*Kind* of?" Ashley whispered loudly.

"I think I have just the brush for it," Kathleen said, reaching toward the items on the table. "And my first tip of the day—so everyone pay attention—is, 'Never apologize for any part of your physical appearance.'" She looked out at the group of girls staring back at her. "Start by loving who you are, and then play up your best features."

By now she had pulled Lily's hair back from her face without tugging so much as a single strand. She picked up a ball of cotton and a bottle of some kind of liquid.

"For instance, not only does Lily have beautiful hair, but she has wonderful, china-white skin. She'll want to take care of it."

There were some more snickers, and again Lily looked at Reni. She was still nodding and dimpling.

Kathleen dabbed the damp cotton ball on Lily's face and continued talking while she spread it around. Lily didn't hear much of what she said because the stuff was cold. She hoped there wasn't going to be a test on this.

"How do you feel, Lily?" Kathleen said.

"Um, revitalized."

"*What?*" Marcie McCleary burst out. She was as bad as Shad sometimes.

There was a spattering of giggles. Kathleen smiled.

"Great word, Lily," she said. "Revitalized is just the feeling I was going for." She turned to the girls. "A gentle cleanser will make your skin feel alive and refreshed." She reached for a bottle of creamy stuff and applied a light amount to Lily's cleansed face as she continued talking. "At this point in your lives, a good facial wash, a gentle liquid cleanser and toner like this, and a light moisturizer with sunscreen are all you need to be beautiful. Look at Lily—she's lovely."

Lily wished she could put her hands over her ears. Not only were they turning red too, but she didn't want to hear the comments from Ashley and Chelsea and Marcie.

The room was quiet, though, and Lily sneaked a look. In the second row, tiny Suzy Wheeler was nodding her head, and so was Zooey Hoffman.

"What do you know about lovely, Zooey?" Ashley said.

"I'll tell you what *I* know about lovely." Kathleen's voice wasn't so light and airy now. It made them all freeze in their seats and look at the floor. "Lovely is a woman who does not make mean remarks about anyone else. She appreciates the beauty every female has."

Kathleen's eyes swept the library. It was quiet as midnight. The only person who moved was Zooey. She pulled her plump self up tall in her chair and smiled at Lily out of a round, cherry-cheeked face. Lily smiled back.

Marcie raised her hand. "Don't we get to see anything about makeup?" she said.

"As I told you, good clean skin and some moisturizer are all you really need, but I will admit that makeup is fun to experiment with. Lily, would you mind if I tried a little blush on you?"

"Yeah!" a bunch of the girls said.

Lily didn't look to see if Ashley was one of them. She felt good all of a sudden, and she didn't want to spoil it.

"Sure," Lily said. "Only not too much. I don't think my parents would like it."

"I would never go against anything parents say," Kathleen said. "We'll put on just enough to see how you'll look, and then you can wipe it right off if you want."

She tickled Lily's cheeks with a big fluffy brush and stood back to observe.

"Wow—that looks good!" Marcie said. "Can you do me, please?"

"I'm not finished with Lily yet," Kathleen said. "Would you mind a little lip gloss, Lily?"

A little? On these lips, you're going to need a whole container.

Kathleen seemed to be watching her closely. "You have incredible lips, you know. Women all over America are going to plastic surgeons to get lips like yours."

"Nuh-uh!" Ashley said, and then clapped her hands over her mouth.

"It's true. We'll apply some gloss just to play up that wonderful mouth, okay?"

Lily nodded and then closed her eyes while Kathleen put something smooth and cool on her lips. When she opened her eyes, she saw Reni smiling from one earlobe to the other.

"Lily!" Marcie said. "You look *good!*"

She sounded like that was the surprise of the century, but Lily didn't mind. The girls were all murmuring to each other and casting the same kinds of glances at Lily. She was dying for a mirror.

"Now," Kathleen said, "you will notice that we haven't done anything to change Lily's appearance. We're just enhancing what she has. Do you know what *enhancing* means?"

Ashley stuck up her hand. "It means making something look good that didn't look that good before."

"Absolutely not correct," Kathleen answered briskly. "Anyone else?"

It took a minute before anyone else raised her hand. Lily was surprised when Kresha Ragina put hers up. Kresha didn't speak English that well—she was Croatian—so she hardly ever answered in class.

Kathleen nodded in her direction. "Yes, pretty lady." Frankly, Lily had never thought of Kresha as pretty. She seldom combed her tangle of almost-blond hair, and matching colors was obviously something they didn't worry about too much in Croatia.

Wow, Lily thought, *Kathleen really does look for each person's own beauty.*

Kresha cleared her throat. "It mean . . . to make you notice . . . what—what . . . um . . . what is beautiful already."

"Beautifully put," Kathleen said. "And exactly right. Caking on a bunch of makeup doesn't make you beautiful. You are already beautiful. If you wear makeup, it is only to make people notice your best qualities." She turned back to Lily. "Now, another way to do that is with color. Lily, would you mind if I put something over the top you're wearing?"

Lily looked down at her black T-shirt and shook her head. Kathleen reached into her classy bag and pulled out several scarves in different colors.

"I'm going to hold each one of these up to Lily's face," she told the class, "and I want you girls to tell me which one brings out Lily's beauty the best."

By now, almost everyone had scooted to the front

of her chair, eyes glued to Lily. Kathleen held a yellow scarf over Lily's tee, and only a few heads nodded. With a red one, heads shook. When blue, just the color of Lily's eyes, covered her, Lily thought Marcie McCleary was going to spring out of her chair.

"That's the one!" she said.

"What do you think?" Kathleen asked Zooey.

"That's it," Zooey said.

"I totally agree." Kathleen knotted the scarf casually in the front, and then finally she reached into her bag and pulled out a mirror. "Take a look at yourself, Lily," she said. "See if you like what you see."

Lily gazed into the mirror, and she saw her eyes go wide. *It's me, all right*, she thought. *Only it's like a different degree of me.*

"Do you like yourself?" Kathleen said.

"I do."

"You should. You are a lovely young woman. Now—"

"Do me!" Marcie cried. Surely she was going to burst a blood vessel any minute.

Kathleen gave a sly smile. "Did I say I was finished with Lily yet? Now then, Lily, stand up for me. Everyone stand up."

They all scrambled to their feet, buzzing to each other, and Kathleen told them to stand with their arms at their sides, to place their feet the same distance apart as their shoulders, and to focus on an eye-level spot on the wall.

"Concentrate on your backbone," she said. "Pretend those vertebrae in there are Legos. Stack each one neatly above the one below it."

There was a lot of giggling and whispering from the

other girls, but Lily put her mind to her Legos, snapping each one carefully into place. She was amazed at how different she felt.

"Excellent, Lily," Kathleen said. "Everyone look up here."

Necks stretched again.

"Lily looks so elegant and confident, doesn't she?"

Ashley and Chelsea both shrugged, but some of the others nodded. Reni, of course, dimpled all the way through.

"How do you feel, Lily?" Kathleen said.

"I don't feel like a giraffe right now."

Ashley spewed out a laugh that sprayed everyone in front of her, but Kathleen ignored her.

"Good answer," she said, "because you certainly don't look like one either."

Kathleen showed them how to walk without falling over their own feet and how to stand and not feel like they didn't know where to put their arms, keeping Lily at the front to use as an example. The rest of the class went way too fast as far as Lily was concerned.

By the time the workshop was over, Chelsea had stopped laughing at her. Ashley had too, but she'd also quit listening to Kathleen and was yawning and looking at the clock and re-braiding her hair. By that time, Lily had pretty much forgotten all about her.

When Ms. Gooch came into the library to get them, nobody wanted to leave, and Kathleen had to help her shoo everybody toward the door. But when Lily went up to give Kathleen her blue scarf back, Kathleen took hold of her arm.

"Can you stay for a minute, Lily?" she asked. "I want to give you something."

"You don't need to give me anything," Lily said. "It was fun helping you."

"It's not a thank-you gift." Kathleen opened Lily's hand and pressed a cream-colored card into it. "This is my phone number at the agency. You're model material, and I'd love it if you would tell your mother I said that and have her call me. We'll be starting a new class soon, and I'd like to have you in it."

"Me?" Lily felt her face doing that blotchy-red thing again. "Oh, this is because I was your example. Really, it won't hurt my feelings if you give it to Reni or even Ashley. They're way prettier—"

Kathleen laughed her feathery laugh as she pressed Lily's fingers closed over the card. "No. I'm giving you this because *you* are the one I'd like to have at my agency."

It was way too hard to believe. That was why when Lily got outside the library, and Reni said, "What did she say to you?" Lily just said, "She thanked me. Come on. We better hurry or we'll get our names on the board."

Then Lily tucked the card into the pocket of her jeans—and tucked the warm glow she was feeling into the back of her mind, where she could bring it out later and feel it again.

Three

Lily did think about Kathleen and the card later, when she was setting the table for dinner. The thoughts were nice, but they didn't drown out the usual commotion that was going on in the kitchen.

"Outside with that, Joe," Mom told Lily's nine-year-old brother, who was bouncing a basketball on the tile and rattling the dishes in the cabinets in the process.

"Hey, Art, go for a lay-up!" Joe called out. He motioned toward the hanging onion basket and tossed the ball to Lily's older brother.

Art looked up from the basket he was dropping bread into and smacked the ball away. It bounced off the corner of the counter and hit Lily squarely on the right fanny cheek.

"Mo-om!" Lily said.

"Mo-om!" Joe echoed her.

"Joseph." Mom spoke without raising her voice or even looking up from the salad she was dumping out of its plastic bag into bowls. "I said take that outside."

"Good shot," Joe said to Art as he dribbled the basketball toward the back door.

"That wasn't a shot," Mom said. "It was pure luck,

and it would have been *bad* luck if you'd knocked those glasses off the counter. Speaking of which, Joe, after you get rid of that ball, come back in and put milk in them."

"It would have been bad if he'd knocked the glasses off with the ball, but you don't yell at him for hitting *me* with it?" Lily said.

"He got you in the rear end," Joe teased. "Not that there's much of it, Stick Girl."

"Mo-om!" Lily wailed again.

"I'll give him twenty lashes after dinner," Mom said. "Check the casserole, would you?"

Still mumbling to herself, Lily opened the oven and peered in. "What's it supposed to be doing?"

"The polka." Art started out of the kitchen. "Call me when dinner's on. I'll be in my room."

"Stay here. We're close," Mom told him. "If you go into that cave, we might not see you for hours."

"I could play a whole song before Klutz even gets the casserole to the table."

Lily almost opened her mouth to protest, but it was then that she thought about the card in her pocket. For a moment, she thought she could actually feel its warmth in there. She *wasn't* a gangly giraffe. Kathleen had said so.

"Lily, how come you're smiling into the oven?" Joe said from the doorway.

"Because she's weird," Art said. "Just call me, okay, Mom?"

Mom tilted her head back and shouted, "Art! Dinner's ready!"

"You're so witty, Mother."

"Did somebody say *dinner*?" Lily's father poked his

head into the kitchen, a book dangling from one hand and his glasses from the other. Like Lily's, his red hair was standing up on end, but his blue-like-Lily's eyes weren't sharp and intense at the moment. They had that foggy look to them they *always* had when he'd been off in book-land. Which was usually.

Joe squinted his own brown doe-eyes. "False alarm, Dad," he said. "Mom was being cute."

"Oh." Dad started to leave, putting his glasses back on, already halfway into the pages of his book again.

"Sit down at the table, hon," Mom told him. "It's all but ready. How's it doing, Lil?"

"I don't know," Lily said.

"So ask it," Joe said.

"Is it bubbly and turning brownish on top?" Mom said.

"Yeah."

"Then it's a done deal. Art, come back here and take that out for Lily."

Art gave an exaggerated sigh from the doorway he'd almost sneaked out of. "Why can't she do it?"

"Because I asked you to do it. Joe, wash your hands. Lily, don't forget salad dressings."

"No, it's because she's a klutz." Art snatched the pot holders from their hook.

Lily flung open the refrigerator door—making the wipe-off calendar, with October already filled up, swing on its little hook—and almost started wailing for her mom. But then she patted the card, poked her head inside the fridge, and pulled out the blue cheese and the ranch in silence.

"Watch it, Dad," Art said as he set the bubbling casserole on the table. "She's in a mood."

"Who, Lilliputian?"

"Who else? I think her hormones are getting ready to kick in."

"Arthur, enough." Mom still didn't raise her voice, but her brown eyes said about as much as a whole website as she cut them in his direction.

Art just grinned and parked himself in his chair at the table.

"Why do you call her that anyway?" Joe said from the sink, where he was going through the motions of washing his hands.

"Call who what?" Art said. "Lily, pass the salad."

"*After* we all sit down and *after* we ask the blessing." Mom turned Joe back to the sink and handed him the soap, then got out the milk and set it soundly next to his elbow on the counter.

"Okay, okay," Joe said, barely moving his lips.

Lily put the salad dressing bottles on the table and slid into her seat next to Dad. It was going to be at least another five minutes before everybody did everything they were supposed to do and got to their places. She used that time to study her family.

What would Kathleen do with them? she wondered.

Mom had her brown sugar–colored hair pulled up on top of her head in a ponytail, and there was definitely no makeup on her big brown eyes or her tan face or her twitchy little mouth. Lily's mom didn't smile that much, but she wasn't serious either. She said funny things with a straight face, and her lips were always threatening to burst into a laugh but almost never did. Lily was sure Kathleen would have replaced the gray Cedar Hills High School Coaching Staff sweatshirt with one of her scarves—*if* she could have gotten the shirt off Mom. She was pretty proud of her girls' volleyball team.

Lily shifted her attention to Dad, who was reading the back of the blue cheese dressing bottle. He was a taller, male version of Lily, except that he wore glasses and wasn't clumsy. Of course, Lily didn't think a person had to be too coordinated to teach English literature to college students.

Art, she decided, looked like the two of them too, only he had Mom's brown-like-a-deer's eyes, and his hair was brown with just a tinge of red instead of looking like a bumper crop of carrots. His was also wild-curly, but he kept it cut very short so no one ever accused *him* of looking like he was about to take flight. Lily had often almost wished she could shave hers off the way he did, but after today with Kathleen, she was glad she hadn't. Her hair might not be so bad after all.

Joe and Art haven't said anything hateful about it all afternoon, she thought. *I bet they've noticed that there's something different about me, only they can't figure out what yet.*

Joe finally finished filling the milk glasses and got them and himself to the table. Lily surveyed him carefully. He was definitely the best-looking one in the family. He had Mom's smooth hair and her big brown eyes and her golden-bronze complexion. He'd gotten Dad's huge mouth and full lips, but they kind of worked on him, maybe because his face was wider. He never looked as if his smile were going to go off his face and meet in the back of his head, the way hers did.

Except Kathleen said I have a great mouth and great lips, Lily reminded herself.

"What are you starin' at?" Joe said. "Mom, make Lily quit starin' at me. She's weirdin' me out."

"Your turn to ask the blessing, hon," Mom said.

They all held hands, and Dad thanked God for the food and for their family and asked Him to guide them through life. Lily added her usual silent, *And please help my brothers not to pick at me*, and then put in, *And thank You for Kathleen.*

"Amen."

"*Lilliputian*," Dad said, "is a reference to the book *Gulliver's Travels*."

They all looked blankly at Dad.

"What's he talking about?" Art said to Mom.

"Joe asked why I call Lily *Lilliputian*. It's a literary allusion."

"Great," Art said. "Pass the salad."

"In the land of the Lilliputians," Dad went on, "Gulliver found the people to be extremely small."

"Then I still don't get why you call *her* that," Joe said. "Lily's, like, way tall."

"She's a beanpole," Art said. "What do I have to do to get the salad around here?"

"You have to stop being rude," Lily said. She was trying to think about the card in her pocket and not let Art make her yell, but it was getting harder. "And I am not a beanpole."

"What is a beanpole anyway?" Joe asked. "I don't get that."

"Something tall and thin like your sister," Mom said. "Elbows, Joe."

Joe removed his elbows from the table and smiled at Lily like a little imp. "Does it have a big mouth?"

Lily gritted her teeth.

"Did he just ask if a beanpole has a mouth?" Dad asked, blinking behind his glasses.

Mom's lips twitched. "It isn't that Lily's mouth is so big. It's just that her face is so small."

Art stopped pouring ranch dressing onto his salad to look at Lily. "Nah," he said. "Her mouth's just big."

"Mo-om!" Card or no card, Lily couldn't help herself.

Dad put his fork down and reached over to squeeze the back of Lily's neck with his warm Daddy-hand. "Ignore them, Lilliputian," he said. "You know we love you no matter what you look like."

Lily shook herself away from her father and scraped her chair back from the table.

"You know what?" she said as she stuck her hand into her pocket. "You're all wrong! A lady from a modeling agency came to our school today, and she said I was model material!" She pulled out the card and shoved it into Art's face. "So there!"

Four

A rt snatched the card from her. "This is fake."

"It is not! Mo-om! Make him give it back."

Somehow Mom got the card from Art, and Dad made him *and* Joe "cut Lily some slack" for the rest of the meal, and both her parents promised they would talk about Kathleen and the modeling agency later.

Since "later" had been known to stretch into "never," Lily brought it up again as soon as the kitchen was cleaned up, before Dad could disappear into his study. She caught them both in the family room, where Mom was folding laundry and Dad was looking for a pen, and told them all about it.

"Sounds like it was fun for you," Mom said when Lily was finished. "I personally would have hated it, but then you're nothing like me—and that's okay," she added quickly. "You know we want you to be exactly who God made you to be."

"So will you call her?" Lily said.

"Why exactly does she want to talk to your mother?" Dad held up a blue pen. "Ah, here it is! How did it wind up under somebody's sweatpants? Whose pants are these anyway?"

"She says she wants me in her next class," Lily said.

"I see." Mom scowled at some unpaired socks. "Does that dryer eat our socks, do you think?"

"So can I?"

Mom looked at Dad, but he gave her the this-one's-up-to-you shrug. "Hon." Mom touched Lily's arm gently. "I have a feeling the lady is trying to drum up business for her school. I don't mean to burst your bubble, but that could be why she gave you her card."

"Then why didn't she give everybody cards?" Lily said. "They were practically begging her to, but she only gave one to me."

"Oh."

"She has a point," Dad said.

"But I've never known you to have an interest in modeling before," Mom said. "We don't know how much this is going to cost, and for something you just suddenly decided you wanted to do . . ."

"I don't *know* if I want to do it," Lily said. "But she said I'd be good at it. If Art wanted to try a new instrument he'd never played before, you'd let him do it."

"He's a musician," Dad said. "We established that when he was five years old."

"And if Joe wanted to play another sport, you'd sign him up."

"He's an athlete—"

"But what am I?"

"You're—"

Mom stopped shaking out jeans and looked at Dad. He was chewing on the earpiece of his glasses.

"See?" Lily said. "Nobody knows. I don't even know! I want to have a 'thing' just like all of you do."

Her parents exchanged more looks, and Lily bit her lip to keep from nagging. That was one sure way to get your whole case thrown out. Finally, Dad cleared his throat, and Mom nodded.

"All right," Mom said. "I'll call her and get the particulars, but we're not promising anything."

"Will you call her now?" Lily said. "The phone number's on the card."

Mom sighed and pushed the laundry basket toward her. "I can see there will be no rest until I do it. Finish folding those for me, would you?"

"You might have to describe me to her," Lily called after her. "Just in case she doesn't remember me."

"Oh, don't worry about that," Dad said.

❖

Mom was back in five minutes and announced that Saturday afternoon they'd all be going to a meeting at the agency for prospective models and their parents where they'd get the answers to all their questions.

"You'll have some kind of interview," Mom explained. "Then they'll decide if they want you, and we'll decide if we *want* them to want you—or something like that. Now can we drop it between now and then, or are you going to drive us crazy until we get there?"

"I'll drop it," Lily said.

But she didn't "drop it" from her own head. She could think of almost nothing else until Saturday.

She used her half hour on the computer she had to share with Joe to look up the Rutledge Modeling Agency. All the girls on the website seemed so perfect that she couldn't imagine herself fitting in. Still, Kathleen *had* invited her. Maybe she would look like them when she was done.

When she wasn't memorizing the website, she e-mailed Reni. Called Reni. She would have texted her too, if she'd had a cell phone.

Lily did tell Reni about the modeling thing, of course, and they whispered about it at school every chance they got—a fact that didn't escape Shad Shifferdecker. It suddenly seemed like every time they put their heads together, Shad appeared with his hand cupped around his ear.

At Friday afternoon recess, the two girls were sitting against the fence in the corner farthest from the building under the only tree on the playground. It finally looked like they were safely out of Shad's earshot, so they didn't whisper as they picked up gold- and rust-colored leaves from the ground and made confetti out of them while they talked.

"I *so* can't wait until Saturday," Lily said. "Only . . . I'm a little freaked out. What if they don't want me after they talk to me?"

"Why wouldn't they want you?" Reni said. "Kathleen already said you were beautiful."

"I don't know—"

But Lily never got to finish the sentence. Something suddenly dropped out of the branches over their heads and hit the ground in front of them with a heavy thud. It obviously wasn't an autumn leaf.

Reni screamed. Lily jumped up, grabbed a stick, and held it over her head, ready to pound whatever it was. She'd learned a few things growing up with two brothers.

But she stopped with the stick in midswing. "Shad

Shifferdecker!" she said, gritting her teeth. "You were spying!"

Shad picked himself up from the dirt and brushed some of it off his huge T-shirt, which hung down to his knees. The boys weren't allowed to wear clothes seven sizes too big to school, but Shad somehow got away with it. She was pretty sure that underneath, the waistband of his jeans hung down that far too, and his boxer shorts were probably sticking up above them like he was a gangster or something. The thought of it was disgusting.

"Big deal," Shad said, beady little eyes snapping. "You didn't say nothin' I was interested in. Me? I hang out at the mall on Saturdays."

"Doing what?" Reni said.

"Anything I want."

"And your mom lets you?"

"My mom doesn't 'let' or 'not let' me do anything. I'm practically on my own now."

Lily felt her lip curl. She couldn't have cared less what Shad did on Saturdays. He could be out robbing convenience stores for all she gave a rip. What she *did* care about was how much of their conversation he'd heard, and how much he would carry back to Leo and Daniel so they could get in her face about it later.

"It isn't nice to eavesdrop on other people's conversations," Lily said.

Shad smiled, and his braces glittered in the sun. "I *dropped* all right. You didn't even know I was up there. Duh! I heard everything you said for the last hour."

"We haven't even been here an hour," Reni said.

Lily folded her arms across her chest so she'd appear casual. "What did we say then?"

"Somethin' about bein' all freaked about goin' some-place Saturday." His voice went up into a high pitch. "'What if they don't want me?'" Shad gave a grunt of a laugh. "What's goin' on? Are your parents putting you up for adoption or something?"

"None of your business," Lily said. But she was relieved. At least he hadn't heard them talking about the modeling agency.

"I can tell you exactly what's gonna happen on Saturday," Shad said. "Whoever 'they' are, they're not gonna like you."

"You just hush up your mouth, Shad," Reni said. She stretched her neck up about as far as it would go. "You don't even know anything."

"I know they're not gonna like her," Shad said again, "because nobody likes her. She's too stuck-up."

"You are such a liar," Reni said.

Shad looked at Lily like he was waiting for her to start yelling too. But her face was stinging, and she knew if she said anything, she'd start crying. Shad got even more evil when he managed to make somebody bawl.

Lily hugged her arms in closer to her chest and turned on her heel and walked away, tossing her hair as hard as it would toss. Behind her, Shad grunted several times, his version of a laugh. Reni hurried to catch up with her.

"Don't pay any attention to him," she whispered to Lily.

"I won't," Lily said. Yeah. Like *that* was even possible.

❋

Finally the next day came, and Lily was ready hours before it was time to leave for the Rutledge Agency. She parked herself on the loveseat in the entranceway of their house, dressed in her newest flouncy skirt and the only tunic top that had escaped the day Art did the laundry and washed everything in hot water. Art stopped on his way past and asked her if she was waiting for a bus.

She kind of hoped they would take Dad's little Honda Accord instead of the van Mom always drove. Dad didn't cart kids around. Mom did, which was why the van always had sticky yogurt spoons on the seats, sported really old Fruit Loops on the floor, and smelled like Joe's dirty socks.

I don't want to go into the Rutledge Agency smelling like Joe, Lily wanted to protest. But as they climbed into the van, she heard Dad say, "Tell me again why we're doing this?" So she decided to keep that to herself.

When they got to the agency, it was obvious that other people were close to freaking out too. The meeting room was filled with mothers and fathers and girls who had apparently spent as much time in front of the mirror as Lily had. From the looks of the curls and outfits and even lipstick on a couple of the girls, some had even primped longer. Lily immediately wished she had some of that blush and lip gloss Kathleen had put on her.

What really surprised Lily was that a few boys came too. One of them, who was wearing very cool jeans and had shiny nut-colored hair hanging down over his eyes like Justin Bieber, walked past her, looked back over his shoulder, and started to laugh.

What's so funny? Lily wanted to say to him. She felt her nostrils to be sure nothing was hanging out of them.

Just then, Kathleen stepped up to a microphone at

a podium and asked everybody to have a seat. Lily followed her parents to three seats in the second row. She
stifled a groan when she saw that Cool Jeans was sitting
right in front of them. His mother ran her hand over
his head to smooth his hair, and he pulled away from
her with a jerk.

Evil child, Lily thought. Why did there always have
to be boys? Life would be so much easier without them.

"Welcome, all of you!" Kathleen said into the microphone. "I hope you'll all take a moment to look around
the room because the young people you see here are
very special."

Lily glanced around, and her heart sank. They *were*
better looking than your average kid. She felt like a
giraffe again.

"The reason they're special," Kathleen went on, "is
because I handpicked them from the schools I've been
visiting over the past few weeks."

Lily saw Cool Jeans flip his hair around importantly.

"But not all of you will be invited to join our next
beginners' class," Kathleen said. "We're here today to tell
you about the agency to see if you want us, and we're
here to see if you are the kind of person we would like to
work with." Her eyes went right to Cool Jeans. "We'll be
watching to see how you treat other people, for instance.
If we see that you're going to put other people down to
make yourself feel better, we won't ask you to come back."

She still didn't move her eyes from the kid in the
jeans. Lily could see him squirming. "We may ask some
of you if you would be willing to do certain things, such
as cut your hair so we can see your eyes."

When Kathleen finally looked elsewhere in the

room, Cool Jeans whispered to his father, "No way! I'm not cuttin' my hair!"

Lily let out a long breath and leaned easily back in her chair. *I like it here*, she thought. *I really want to come to this class.*

After she told them about the Rutledge Agency, Kathleen said she was going to go into her office. Her assistant, Tess, would call each one of them back, and she wanted them to come into her office and introduce themselves.

"Then what do we do?" someone asked.

"Nothing," Kathleen answered. "That's it. That's the interview."

When she left the meeting room, the room was one big whisper.

"You mean I got you all dolled up for that?" said a mother across the aisle from the Robbinses. She looked in dismay at her daughter's mass of carefully placed curling-iron curls. "If I'd known that, I would have saved myself the trouble."

"Oh no," said another woman in the row behind them. "That's all the time you get in a real interview for a modeling job. You have to sell yourself in thirty seconds." She sniffed importantly. "My Cassie has the technique down cold."

Lily looked at the girl she assumed was Cassie, who dazzled the group with a toothy smile.

Oh . . . Lily thought, *I don't think I can do that.*

"So what are they looking for?" said one dad. He nudged his now crimson-faced daughter with his elbow. "Listen up, Stinky. This is how you impress the lady."

Stinky? Lily thought. *My whole face would turn into*

a tomato if Dad called me "Lilliputian" in here. I'd croak
if he called me "Stinky."

"You have to make eye contact," the mother behind
them was saying. "And be assertive. Enter and exit
gracefully."

"Uh-oh," Mom whispered to Lily. She grinned. "If you
don't get asked back, Lil, remember that it isn't the end
of the world." She gave Lily a gentle nudge. "Who needs
graceful anyway?"

If that was meant to make Lily feel better, it didn't
work. She turned around and concentrated on not letting
her face get any blotchier than it probably already was.

Tess started calling people's names, and it looked
like the know-it-all mother had been right. Nobody
stayed in the office longer than thirty seconds. Lily's
dad was timing it. Lily was pretty sure that was how he
was staying awake.

When Tess called Lily's name, several people wished
her good luck.

"You're gonna need it," Cool Jeans whispered.

Am I, like, a magnet for absurd little creeps? Lily thought.

She made herself move out of the row without looking at him. The closer she got to Tess, the prouder she
was of her self-control.

Maybe I really do have what it takes to be here, she
thought—until there was a sudden shriek of laughter
from the chairs behind her, a ripple of chuckles, and a
few "Oh dears." Lily looked frantically over her shoulder
to see half the people covering their mouths with their
hands and the other half pointing right at her.

Well, not at her face. At the seat of her skirt.

Lily grabbed at it just as her mother got halfway out

of her chair and whispered loudly between her hands, "Do a fanny check, Lil. I think you brought in some debris from the car."

To her horror, Lily's hand did touch something sticky. When she tried to pull it off, part of it stayed there, and part of it stuck stubbornly to her hand.

Her face, she knew, was one big blotch as she twisted around to examine the back of her skirt. A large wad of grape gum—already *chewed* grape gum—hung from her seat and was connected by an ever-growing string to her fingers.

"You must be Lily," someone whispered near her ear.

Lily looked up to see Tess at her elbow, but she couldn't say anything except, "Gum."

"Don't worry about it," Tess whispered. "Kathleen told me about you. Just go in and be yourself." She winked. "It's a piece of cake."

"But . . . shouldn't I go get this off?"

Tess shook her head. "Pretend it isn't there."

By now Lily was no longer hearing the smothered laughter of the other candidates and their parents. *Pretend it isn't there?* she wanted to scream at this Tess person. *I wish I could pretend I wasn't here!*

For a second she seriously considered making a run for the door and escaping to the parking lot and running for the New Jersey Turnpike. As it was, she looked back again at her parents. Dad was looking bewildered, as if he didn't see what was so funny. Even though her mom was nodding for her to go on, she had her hand halfway over her eyes.

Lily could feel her face going beyond blotchy. She was sure all the color was draining right out of it.

She had to get away from these people and their sick senses of humor, and Kathleen's door was the closest. She went for it.

"Atta girl," Tess whispered. "Stand straight. Focus."

Lily pushed open the door, certain that she was leaving a clothesline of gum behind her. Kathleen looked up at Lily from her desk and smiled.

"Hi," Lily said. "I'm Lily Robbins."

Kathleen put out her hand. Lily stood frozen for a moment, trying to remember which hand she'd touched the gum with. She still couldn't remember as she desperately stuck one in Kathleen's. She nearly fainted on the desk when it came forward clean and gum-less.

"Very nice to see you again, Lily," Kathleen said. "Very nice. You can go on back to the meeting room."

Lily panicked. "Now?"

Kathleen's smile got wider. "Now would be good. Unless you have a question."

I do! How am I going to get out without you seeing this bubblegum plastered all over the back of my skirt?

Lily shook her head and began to back toward the door, feeling behind her for the doorknob. "Thank you," Lily said, still groping. So far she was coming up with only air.

"You're certainly welcome. I'm so glad you came this afternoon. After I talked with your mother, I wasn't sure you would. She seemed to have some reservations. Just a little more to your right, and you'll have it."

"What?"

"If you move a little more to your right, you'll find the doorknob. There you go."

I want to die, Lily thought. *Or at least run for the exit the second I get out of Kathleen's office.* But somehow she managed to get back to her seat between Mom and Dad without bolting from the building.

"I'm sorry, Lil," Mom said. "Really, I am. I'm going to make Joe clean the whole car tomorrow. He's the only one who chews that color."

"Are you going to make him apologize to me for making me lose out on this opportunity?" Lily said.

"Nicely put," Dad said.

"Are you?"

Mom cocked her head at Lily so that her ponytail swung to one side. "If it's meant to be, Lil, it'll be. Frankly, I don't see—"

But just then the microphone squealed, and Kathleen stood in front with a clipboard in her hand.

"I won't prolong the suspense," she said. "Let me just read the names of those young people we are inviting to join our class. Cassie Bauer."

"Now, Lil," Mom whispered, "just remember that some of these kids have been being groomed for this since the high chair—"

"Lilianna Robbins."

"That's me!" Lily said. "I made it!"

Mom looked at Dad, and he took off his glasses and chewed on the earpiece. Lily didn't like the feeling she was getting.

"I can be in the class, can't I?" Lily said. "I mean, I was picked. I'm special, even with stupid gum on my skirt—"

"You are special," Mom said. "And I don't think you need this class to show you that."

Dad gently squeezed the back of Lily's neck. "We just need to think about it, Lilliputian," he said. "We're not ready to say yes."

Five

It was all Lily could do not to wail, "*Whyyyyyy?*" right there in the Rutledge Agency meeting room. She waited until they got out into the parking lot and said it through very tight teeth.

"Because this whole modeling thing seems too focused on appearance to me," Dad said. "You know Mom and I are always urging you kids to do things that will make God proud of you, things that are part of the work He wants us to do."

"Yeah," Lily said. "But—"

"*But,*" Mom finished for her, "how are you contributing anything to God's kingdom by walking up and down a runway so people will buy the clothes you're wearing?"

Lily's mind felt like her iPod on shuffle; it couldn't find a place to stop. Mom and Dad both leaned against the car and watched her.

"I don't know," she finally said. "I just like it here."

"Why?" Dad said.

"Because . . . I don't know. I just do. I like Kathleen."

"Honey, we aren't going to pay just so you can hang out with Kathleen," Mom said. "We'll have her over for dinner or something."

"But she teaches me stuff. She already has. And I—I don't know. Why can't I do it just because I want to?"

Neither of them answered that question. They only leaned against the car and waited. Lily could feel her throat closing up, feel her teeth wanting to grit together harder and harder. If she didn't say something soon, it was all going to be locked up, and she would never get to come back here, where she felt special and not . . .

"I don't feel ugly when I'm around Kathleen!" she said.

"Oh, Lil!" Mom said. "Why would you ever feel ugly?"

But Dad put his hand on Mom's arm. "I tell you what, Lilliputian," he said. "We'll let you take the class, just because it means so much to you. But we're not going to promise that we'll let you sign on with the agency when you're finished. We want to see if God is in this, so the class may end up being the end of it. Can you deal with that?"

Mom gave him a poke with her elbow, but once again Dad patted her arm. Mom closed her mouth, and that was the end of that "conversation," which was fine with Lily. She flung herself at Dad and wrapped her arms around his neck. He laughed softly, close to her ear.

"Thank you!" she said. "You won't be sorry. I promise. I'll try to be the best one in the class."

"I have no doubt you'll try," Mom said. "You always go all out no matter what you do."

Lily wished more than ever that she had a cell phone. It was torture to have to wait until she got home to call Reni. When she did, Reni squealed as if it were happening to her.

"But you have to promise not to tell anybody else," Lily said.

"How come?"

"Because I don't want Shad Shifferdecker to hear about it."

"Oh yeah. He'd *so* make fun of you."

"Fun? He'd flip completely out."

❀

Of course, come Monday morning, Shad made fun of her anyway, every chance he got.

When their class was in the library, he hissed to her, "Hey, since you're taller than King Kong, can you get me that book on the top shelf?"

And when they were at lunch, he said from down the table, "Don't eat those carrots! Dude, it'll turn your hair orange! Oh, sorry. It already *is* orange."

And when they were working on a Native American mural for their classroom wall, he handed her the beige paint and said, "Here. Paint this on your face so you won't look like a dead person."

Sure, it all made Lily want to holler, "Ms. Goo-ooch!" But then she would think about Kathleen and how un-giraffe-like she felt when she was at Rutledge. Then she would just toss her head away from him and move on.

"She thinks she's all that," she heard Shad say to Daniel. Lily merely smiled to herself—and waited for Tuesday night. That would be her first class with Kathleen.

Tuesday evening finally arrived, and Lily spent an hour getting ready. She pulled her hair back the way Kathleen had at the workshop that day, and since she didn't have any cleanser or toner, she scrubbed her face extra hard so it would sort of tingle like she remembered.

She wished she had some blush and lip gloss, but once the class was all assembled, listening to Kathleen talk, she was glad she didn't.

One of the first things Kathleen said to them was, "Now, this class is not about piling on makeup and doing elaborate things with your hair. This is not a beauty pageant."

"That's good!" somebody said. It was one of the two boys in the group. Lily looked around to make *sure* Cool Jeans wasn't one of them.

"I knew you'd appreciate that," Kathleen said.

Her eyes flickered to Cassie, who was sitting next to Lily. Cassie had her hair done up in a bouquet of curls on top of her head, and she was wearing enough lipstick for every girl in the class. When Kathleen looked at her, Cassie said, "My mom made me put all this stuff on."

Kathleen smiled. "That's why we don't let moms in the room during class."

She went on to tell them that they would have a three-hour class once a week for six weeks. During that time, they would learn the best age-appropriate look for each of them. More important, she said, they would discover ways to be poised and confident and to project themselves as people.

"These are not acting lessons," Kathleen warned them. "When you go out to audition for a modeling job or a commercial, you have about thirty seconds to show them who you are. There is no time for acting. You will learn how to walk in with an air that says, 'I know who I am, and I'm not afraid of what you think of me.'"

I would love *to be able to do that around Shad Shifferdecker*, Lily thought. *This is going to be so cool.*

And then Kathleen announced the coolest part. "At the end of our six weeks together," she told the class, "in late November, we will present a modeling show for parents and friends."

The room immediately buzzed.

"T.J.Maxx will bring in clothes, and you will each choose three outfits to model. By then you'll know how to style your hair to match the look of each outfit, and you will be able to walk down the runway with poise and confidence, selling not only the clothes you're wearing, but who you are as well."

Lily took a deep breath. She wasn't sure how she was ever going to get to that point, but she did know one thing. If she did, she was going to make sure Shad Shifferdecker was there to see it.

❀

"No, you are not!" Reni said when Lily told her the next day. It was afternoon recess, and they were sitting under their favorite tree, which was now even more naked than before. That made it easier to make sure there were no eavesdroppers up in the branches this time. "But I don't see how you're going to get him there."

"I don't either," Lily said. "But I've gotta do it. Can't you just see the look on his face when I pivot at the end of the runway and don't fall off?"

Reni giggled.

Lily had already envisioned it a dozen times. His mouth would be hanging open, his eyes would be wide, and there would be a general look of oh-Lily-you-are-so-gorgeous-I'll-never-tease-you-again on his face. Even his eyebrows would be impressed.

"What's 'pivot'?" Reni said.

"I'll show you."

Lily got up and demonstrated what Kathleen had taught them the night before. She walked slowly, keeping her focus out ahead of her, and then stopped and turned without lowering her eyes to the ground. She was a little wobbly, but she did it much better than her first try in class, when she'd gotten her legs completely tangled and had wound up looking like a pretzel.

"Keep trying, Lily," Kathleen had told her. "It's all about trying."

Lily had gotten it on the next attempt.

Reni's eyes were shining. "Wow. You look like a real model!"

"You could do it. It's easy."

"No it is *not*," Reni said.

But Lily pulled her up by the wrist and gave her the instructions. They were walking side by side, eyes glued to the Dumpster as their focus, when they heard cackling from the direction of the bike racks. Lily looked back long enough to see Ashley and Chelsea perched on top of one.

"What do you think *you're* doing?" Ashley said.

"Lily's showing me—" Reni started to say, but Lily gave her a jab in the rib.

"Showing you what? How to look like a geek?" Ashley said.

Chelsea shrieked out a laugh that was way too loud for something that wasn't that funny. Reni looked at Lily.

"You ought to let me tell them," she said between her teeth. "It'll shut them up so fast!"

Lily shook her head. "She'll tell Shad. I know it. I want this to be a total surprise."

It turned out she was right. A direct line seemed to be tied between Ashley and Shad, because the minute the class was lined up at the water fountain after recess, Shad stepped out of line and walked up and down, staring ahead of him and turning on his toes at the end of each pass.

"What are you doing?" Zooey said.

But Lily knew, and she could feel the blotches forming on her face.

"Guess who I am?" Shad said.

"Goofy," Reni said. "No, wait! Pluto." She rolled her eyes practically up into her head and got Zooey laughing, but she also looked nervously at Lily. Lily tried not to grit her teeth.

Shad continued to pace up and down doing spazzy-looking turns, shoulders thrown back and hips swaying. "Guess again!" he said.

"A robot playing basketball!" Leo said.

"No!"

"Somebody walking in their sleep!" Marcie said.

"No!"

"Yes, it is," she said. "Your eyes are all staring, but you aren't seeing anything. That's the way it is when you walk in your sleep. My mother says I do it all the time and—"

"I oughta know what I'm doing." Shad bared his metal-speckled teeth.

"Who are you, then?" Marcie said.

Shad stopped, and to Lily's horror, he pointed straight at her. "I'm doing my Lily Snobbins imitation!"

"Lily *Snobbins!*" Leo cried. "Yeah!"

He high-fived Shad and Daniel snorted, and Lily felt her face blotches turn into one big mass of red. Behind her, she heard cackling. When she looked back, Ashley and Chelsea had their mouths buried in their sleeves. Their eyes were laughing meanly, right at her.

Right then, it was impossible for Lily to keep her arms at her sides, her feet planted firmly hip-distance apart, and her eyes focused on a point in front of her. She didn't feel poised or confident or any of those Kathleen things. She just felt like a giraffe.

"It doesn't take all afternoon to get drinks of water," Ms. Gooch called out from the double doors. "What's the holdup?"

"Shad was—" Marcie started to say.

But Ms. Gooch held up her hand and said, "Shad, back in line," and then watched with one eyebrow up.

Nothing more was said about the "Lily imitation." But Lily couldn't forget. Now there was no doubt about it: she *had* to get Shad Shifferdecker to that modeling show. And she only had six weeks to figure out how.

Six

For the next few weeks, most of Lily's thoughts were tied up with the modeling class, not with Shad. She had so many things to learn.

Kathleen spent one whole session on what was called "slating," where they had to look into a video camera and introduce themselves.

"Look at the camera, not at the operator," Kathleen told them. "Speak with expression. You have thirty seconds to sell yourself to the casting director."

That night, whenever Lily wasn't taking her turn with the camera, she was in front of a mirror, practicing.

In another session, they worked on perfecting their runway walk. After Lily's mom bought her the required slick-bottomed shoes, pivoting was easier, but she still practiced every day on the hardwood floors at home.

"Mom, she's wearin' a path," Art would say, but Lily just kept pivoting.

One of her favorite exercises in class was when Kathleen would give each person a question to answer while slating. If there was one thing Lily could do, it was find the right words—for any subject.

"You express yourself beautifully, Lily. That will be a

great asset to you." Kathleen smiled and rested a smooth, manicured hand on Lily's arm. "But remember, you only have thirty seconds." Lily had rattled on for a good ninety.

Still, Kathleen was always giving Lily compliments.

The night they practiced for their photo shoot, she told Lily that she was very photogenic. "The camera loves you" were her exact words.

The night Cassie showed up in ripped jeans, Kathleen used Lily as an example of how she wanted them to look for class. "Lily looks professional in this dress," she said to the group. "She's putting her best foot forward. Your grubbies are great in their place, but going out for a modeling job is *not* that place."

Even the night they practiced walking out of a room without turning their backs to anyone *in* the room, Lily was Kathleen's model.

"You've done this before," she whispered to Lily with a tiny smile. Then she turned to the class and said, "Notice how Lily keeps her attention on the person at the desk, not on herself? When you're not thinking so much about yourself, you tend to move more gracefully. It's self-consciousness that makes us trip over things." She then pretended to fall over a chair, and everyone laughed. Lily just glowed. The whole gum-on-the-skirt episode had been erased.

The last fifteen minutes of every session, the parents were allowed to come in and watch them demonstrate what they'd learned that night. Lily liked that part. She always pretended that Shad was part of their tiny "audience" and that he was totally blown away by her presence.

"I was right," Mom said on the third night, when she and Lily were headed for Maggie Moo's after class.

"About what?" Lily said.

"You are going all out for this."

"I want to be the best," Lily said.

Mom licked thoughtfully at the drippy edge of her cone. "Have you figured out where God is in it yet?"

"No." Lily swallowed hard. "I forgot about that."

"I see."

"So . . . how's your volleyball team doing?" Lily asked quickly. "Do you think they'll make it all the way to State?"

Mom gave her a long look that clearly said, *Since when are you interested in how my volleyball team is doing?* But then she took another lick of chocolate from her cone and said, "I think they will. Thanks for asking. The tournament's in three weeks."

Lily promised herself she'd think more about the God part. But it was sure easier to think about ways to be even better in Kathleen's class.

She packed away all her rock and feather collections and decorated her room with pictures of teen fashion models who looked "poised and confident."

When she got money for doing extra chores around the house—like reorganizing the linen closet and cleaning the top of the refrigerator and all those other things her parents never had time to do—she spent it on skin care products and fashion magazines and cute shirts in "her" colors. Mom and Dad had entire "eye conversations" about all of it; they agreed she could do it as long as she didn't take her mind off the things she was supposed to be thinking about.

On the night of the actual photo shoot, Lily couldn't think about anything *else*.

They'd been practicing for a couple of sessions on

how to project themselves to the camera, and Lily was ready. She picked out an aqua tunic top that Kathleen said was perfect with her coloring, and since they were just doing head shots, she concentrated on her hair.

Art came by the bathroom when she was in there smoothing it down to fit into two clips, the way Kathleen had shown her.

"If either of those gets loose," he said, "somebody could be killed."

Lily closed the bathroom door.

"Wimp!" Art called through the door. But he didn't sound quite as cocky as usual.

The moms were allowed to come into the classroom at the beginning of the session that night so Kathleen could talk to them about the photo shoot.

"If your son or daughter is going to go for modeling jobs," she explained, "you'll need to have a résumé for him or her, which includes a list of your child's characteristics and experience and an eight-and-a-half-by-eleven color copy of your child's best head shot, plus the digital file. We'll also use that photo for your child's composition card." She held up a card that looked a lot like the baseball cards Joe collected. "It will have a picture on one side and vitals on the other. Sometimes a casting director will flip through a hundred of these and pick out five kids he wants to see in person."

"How can he tell anything from that?" It was Cassie's mother, of course. She had a tube of lipstick in her hand, which she was about to apply to Cassie's lips while Kathleen was talking.

"Most casting directors are searching for a particular look—maybe wholesome all-American or academic, something like that," Kathleen said. "One glance at a photo will tell them if Cassie has that look, but he won't even consider her if she's covered with makeup. He wants to see the child—the talent, as we call it in the business—not the makeup."

Cassie's mother gave a loud sniff and shoved the lipstick back in her purse.

When Kathleen was finished and the moms got up to leave, Lily's mom put her hand firmly on Lily's arm.

"Go ahead and have your picture taken, Lil," she said. "But remember, we don't know yet if you're going to sign with the agency. I don't see the point in buying a bunch of pictures you aren't going to use."

"But I might!" Lily said.

"We'll see." Mom patted Lily's arm and went out to join the other mothers.

Lily knew her face was getting blotchy, and she stayed in her chair waiting for it to go white again. She felt someone sit down beside her.

"That won't be a good look for your photo," Kathleen said softly. "Something with a little more smile to it would be better."

Lily smiled at her, but she didn't feel it inside her.

"What's up?" Kathleen said.

"I don't know if I should have my picture taken. My mom says it might be just a waste of time."

Kathleen didn't look surprised. She definitely didn't get up and march out to the lobby to set Lily's mother straight. She just leaned a little into Lily's shoulder. "Nothing you do here is a waste, Lily," she said. "I've watched you become more poised with every class."

It was as if Lily had just been pumped full of helium.

She floated up off the chair like a balloon and preened and posed and laughed for the camera until even the photographer said, "You're a natural."

❀

Of course, none of Lily's wonderful new qualities seemed to come to Shad Shifferdecker's attention at all. Matter of fact, he seemed to find even more reasons than ever to tease Lily.

"Hey, silly Lily!" he shouted on the playground one day. "How come your lips are so shiny? Did your nose run down on 'em or something?"

Another day when the class was lining up to go to lunch, he got behind her and made a grab for her hair.

Lily bobbed her head away. "What are you doing?" she said.

"I wanna see what'll happen if I take one of these clip things out. I wanna see it go *boi-ing, boi-ing, boi-ing.*" He made a noise like a spring, which made Daniel and Leo practically wet their pants laughing.

"Pretend they don't exist," Reni whispered to her.

But Lily didn't have to be reminded. All she had to do was imagine Shad's face when he saw her flowing down the runway at the modeling show, his eyebrows arched in disbelief, mouth hanging open showing *all* his braces. She still didn't know how she was going to get him there, but the thought made it easy to flip her hair away from him now and smile her way on to lunch.

❀

One day not long after that, Ms. Gooch brought in about twenty boxes of magazines and passed out scissors.

"We're going to do a collage project," she told the class. "We've been reading about great people and their lives this fall, and one of the things we've learned about them is that they each had a vision for their life."

"My dad says people who see visions are weird," Marcie said without raising her hand.

"I'm not asking you to be weird," Ms. Gooch said. "I'm asking you to cut out pictures that say something to you about your vision—or your idea—of your future life, what you want it to be like. You'll assemble them into a collage."

Lily couldn't *wait* to get started on *that* assignment. She didn't even have to think twice about it before she gathered up an armload of fashion magazines and went to work clipping out pictures of women she wanted to look like.

It isn't the makeup and the hair, she reminded herself as she passed up pictures of too-perfect-to-be-real women with blue eyelids and bright red lips. *It's the confidence and the light in their eyes.*

And then she pounced on a photo of a tall, red-haired girl walking along a beach with her dress blowing out behind her and her arms up over her head as if she couldn't care less what anybody thought.

Lily had cut out about thirty similar pictures and was playing with ways to arrange them on a big piece of construction paper when she felt somebody looking over her shoulder.

"That's your 'vision'?" Shad Shifferdecker said.

Lily spread her hands out over her pictures, but Shad reached down and pulled one out from under her fingers. It tore as he yanked it free, and Lily was only fast enough to grab half of it. Shad held the other half up to look at it.

"*This* is what you think you're gonna look like—half a person?"

Lily snatched it from him and looked at it in dismay. "This was one of my favorites!"

She wanted to rip her tongue in half the minute she said it, because Shad's beady gaze began to gleam. Lily was sure his eyes were getting closer together too as he looked down at the rest of her pictures.

"Dream on," he said. "No way you're ever gonna look like *that!*" He picked up a photo of Taylor Swift. "You're too weird lookin' to be her." He poked another picture with a dirty fingernail. "Too snotty to be her, too *ugly* to be her—"

Lily scooped the rest of the pictures together with her forearms and leaned down over them.

"Go. Away." She was grinding her teeth until they hurt. "Please."

She felt a poke in her left rib, but she didn't move. Shad tried another poke, but Lily held her breath and stayed hovered stubbornly over her pile of pictures.

"Snobbins," he said. But he finally moved away.

Lily looked around for Ms. Gooch. She was in the back corner, helping Kresha, who obviously had no idea what they were supposed to be doing and was fingering her tousled hair in frustration as she listened.

I wish Ms. Gooch would yell at Shad, Lily thought fiercely. *I wish she'd tell him he was weird looking and ugly!*

Lily would have done it herself . . . except Kathleen wouldn't have approved.

She sighed and went up to Ms. Gooch's desk to get the tape to repair her prized picture. On the trip up the aisle and back, she got another earful of Shad.

51

"What's *your* vision, Miss Piggy?" he asked Zooey.

"Quit calling me that," Zooey said.

Shad snapped his fingers. "I keep on getting you and her mixed up." Then he puffed out his cheeks and held his arms out to his sides and lumbered on like he weighed two hundred pounds. Lily glanced at Zooey. Her face was hot red, and she was staring down at a magazine.

I know just how you feel, Zooey, Lily wanted to tell her.

"Hot air balloons?" Shad was saying. He was leaning over Suzy's desk now. "You're going to spend your future in a hot air balloon?"

"You're going to spend yours in the office if you don't go to your seat and get to work," Ms. Gooch said. She punctuated it with an eyebrow.

As Shad shrugged and took his sweet time getting to his desk and Suzy slid down into hers and wadded up the balloon picture in her hand, Lily almost cracked her molars.

Don't let him get to you. And you either, Zooey, she wished she could say.

And then Lily un-gritted her teeth and sat up straight in her chair. Why *didn't* she say that to them? What if she did? What if she told Suzy and Zooey and Reni what she was learning from Kathleen? What if they *all* made it impossible for Shad to have anything to tease them about?

It gave her an idea, an idea so good she could hardly wait until lunch to tell them about it.

Seven

$\mathcal{L}$ily gave the playground tree a thorough search with her eyes before she sat down under it with Reni and Suzy and Zooey. Even then, she scanned the entire schoolyard until she saw Shad and Leo and Daniel showing off under the basketball net.

"Huh," Reni said, following Lily's gaze with hers. "They sure think they're all that, don't they?"

Zooey's face went scarlet at the sight of them. "I wish that Shad Shifferdecker would get hit in the face with the ball," she said.

Suzy gave a nervous giggle, but there was no laughter in her eyes.

"*I* wish the ball would go right down his throat," Reni put in. "Maybe *that* would shut him up."

"I have a better idea." Lily wiggled her eyebrows.

Suzy looked up from her lap. "Is it going to get us in trouble? I'm not allowed to get in trouble at school."

"Nope," Lily said. "This is all legal. I want us to form a club."

The three of them blinked at her . . . and then they all began talking at the same time.

"What kind of club?"

"Like Girl Scouts or something?"

"What good's that gonna do?"

Lily put up both hands and both eyebrows to quiet them down.

"Wow," Zooey said. "You look just like Ms. Gooch when you do that."

"What do you mean, a club?" Reni asked. "Like some kind of secret society or something?"

"Aren't those against the rules?" Suzy said.

"Would you guys just listen?" Lily said.

Three heads nodded.

"Okay. I say we should form a . . . group. Let's call it a group. A *girls only* group. Absolutely no boys allowed."

"I like *that* part," Reni said, frowning toward the basketball court.

"And no mean girls either," Lily added.

"Like Ashley?"

"Or Chelsea?"

"Like anybody who hurts people's feelings," Lily said. "Right now I think it should be just the four of us."

"Why us?" Zooey asked.

Lily gave her a long look and then nodded at the basketball hoop. Zooey blinked at her.

"I get it," Reni said. "We're the ones Shad and those guys pick on."

"Right," Lily said.

"What are we gonna do, fight them?" Zooey said. Her eyes bulged fearfully.

"I don't think I'm allowed to do that," Suzy said.

"That's not what you're thinking, is it?" Reni said to Lily.

Lily shook her head. "Nope. What I'm thinking is that

I've been learning about ways to look better—" She stopped. She'd almost let the secret out. For once she was glad Zooey burst in with—

"You *do* look better!" She gaped openmouthed into Lily's face. "I mean, better than you used to. I mean, not that you *were* ugly."

Lily shrugged. "That's okay. I didn't used to make the most of what I had, but now I do."

"Just like that one lady told us," Suzy said.

Lily gave Reni a quick look, but Reni didn't say a word.

"So," Lily said, "we could form a group, and I could teach you what I've been learning, and then Shad Shifferdecker wouldn't be able to make us lose it when he teases us."

"You think he'd ever *stop* teasing us?" Zooey asked. "That's what *I* want."

Lily thought again of the modeling show, and she smiled. "That could happen," she said. "So, who wants to join?"

Zooey's chubby arm shot right up. Reni raised her hand too. Suzy glanced at both of them and then stuck her arm up and looked at her lap.

"Perfect," Lily said.

"So how do we make a group?" Zooey said.

"We need a name first," Reni said, and then she looked at Lily. "Don't we?"

"We should elect a president first. Then I—she—could run the meeting and pick a name."

"You be the president, Lily," Zooey said. "Since it was your idea."

Lily looked around at the little group, just to be polite, and they all nodded.

"Okay," Lily said, trying not to smile too big. "So who has a suggestion for a name?"

Suzy shook her head and continued to study her knees, and Zooey wrinkled up her forehead and looked stumped.

"Girls Only Group," said Reni. "Just like you said."

"That's a little boring," Lily responded. "I mean, no offense."

Reni pulled in her chin that way she had and said, "Huh!"

"Okay, I guess that's good," Lily said. "Only maybe we could spell *girls* with a *z*."

"Zirls?" Zooey said. The furrows in her forehead got deeper.

"No. G-i-r-l-z," Lily said patiently.

"That'll look good on our T-shirts," Reni said.

Zooey's eyes lit up. "We get T-shirts?"

"Well, not right away—"

"Maybe not ever," Lily said. "This *is* a secret group."

"Isn't secret bad?" Suzy said.

"We just don't want Shad and them finding out about it," Lily said. "They'd think it was lame and make fun of it."

Reni nodded. "I get it. But he's gonna know something's up. Look at him right now."

All their heads turned toward Shad, who was standing, ball poised on his hip, staring right at them and saying something to Leo and Daniel out of the side of his mouth.

Suzy giggled her nervous giggle. "Maybe we should just split up before he comes over here."

"I think we should find another place to meet," Reni said.

"I guess so," Lily said. "But we can't hide around here. He'd turn it into his mission in life to find us."

"Wow." Zooey blinked at her. "You always talk so smart. How do you do that?"

"So who says we have to meet at school?" Reni said. "We could meet *after* school, like at Lily's."

Lily shook her head. "Not with my brothers hanging around. They're worse than Shad and Leo and Daniel all in one."

They gave a group shudder and were silent. Lily saw Shad and his two sidekicks moving closer.

"Wait . . . I got it!" Reni said. "Lily, you know that playhouse in my backyard where we used to play dolls and stuff?"

"Yeah."

"My mom's about to turn it into a gardening shed or something. But if I told her I still wanted to use it, we could have it for our clubhouse."

"Cool!" Zooey almost shouted.

It *was* a cool idea, especially with Shad and Leo and Daniel moving in for the kill.

"Okay. Today after school. Reni's backyard," Lily whispered. "We'll pick up there where we left off. Now, everybody—scatter!"

Suzy was the first one to bolt. Reni grabbed Lily's hand, and they scampered off toward the volleyball court. Zooey went right past Shad, but fortunately Shad seemed too disappointed to remember to hurl any insults at her. Lily glanced over her shoulder to see him standing, arms crossed over his chest, looking at her and Reni.

"I think we have him going already," Lily whispered.

✤

So the first official meeting of the Girlz Only Group took place that very afternoon in Reni's old playhouse. They decided to set aside all other business until they could get rid of the dolls-having-a-tea-party décor. They spent that whole afternoon packing up the doll furniture and running to their own houses to bring back posters and cushions their moms didn't want anymore and anything else un-little-girlish they could find.

Suzy brought a bunch of long strings of beads, which they hung in the doorway to provide even more privacy than just the thin front door.

Zooey donated an ancient CD player that only played CDs but didn't fast-forward between tracks anymore. Lily thought that was okay—it still played their faves and was louder than her iPod so everybody could hear.

Reni found a bright pink rug her mother had bought for their bathroom on sale and ended up hating but couldn't return to the store.

"It sure is *pink*," Suzy said, giggling.

"It makes a statement though," Lily said. "We're Girlz. We need a strong pink that says that."

Zooey gazed at her in admiration. "Wow," she said.

When they all stood back to gaze at the finished product, Lily was amazed at how, well, *sophisticated* it looked. If Shad Shifferdecker were to see it, he couldn't say it was lame. Except, of course, that Shad had absolutely no taste whatsoever.

They didn't get to their real purpose—taking away all reasons for Shad to tease them—until two meetings later.

They had to elect the other officers first. Reni was vice president, Suzy was secretary, and since there was no money to keep track of and so no reason for a treasurer, Zooey was given the title of "lookout." It was her job to make sure no boys were spying on them at any time.

Then they had to establish rules. Lily thought they were called "bylaws," but since nobody was really sure, they called them rules. Suzy wrote them down carefully in a special notebook as they were decided.

1. *The Girlz Only Group is totally secret. Nobody else gets to know about it unless everybody says yes.*
2. *We meet every day after school except when somebody has a piano lesson or gymnastics or something.*
3. *We can bring a snack but no big meals.*
4. *Nobody's allowed to say anything to hurt somebody else's feelings because we get enough of that from boys.*
5. *Everybody agrees never to let Shad Shifferdecker or any other boy see that he's getting to us.*

Number two was for Suzy's benefit. She was the only one who had any lessons right after school.

Number three was because of Zooey. Nobody said so, of course, but she always seemed to be carrying the contents of a refrigerator around with her.

Number five—the one about not letting any boy see that he was getting to them—was the hardest one to keep.

✻

They were all at their computers in the classroom the next day, where the space was too small and crowded to begin with, when Zooey accidentally ran into Shad trying to get between some chairs. Shad hurled himself into the next row and said, "Dude! I bounced off!"

Zooey turned scarlet and balled up her fists and opened her mouth, and she probably would have hollered something if Reni and Lily hadn't pushed her into a seat and whispered, "Remember the rule."

Then later, at lunch, Leo peered at Suzy's lunch tray in the cafeteria and asked, "Your mommy still packs you animal crackers?"

Suzy scrunched her shoulders up and hung her face down, almost into her sandwich bag, and Lily and Reni exchanged looks. Suzy was going to be a hard one to change.

But even the two of *them* found it tough to keep their cool when Shad and his buddies turned their attention their way.

"Quick, dude, get me some sunglasses!" Shad shouted when they were outside that afternoon. "Dude, Lily. Yer skin's so white, I can't see with the sun shining on it. Go inside—you're blinding me!"

Then he looked at Reni. "Hey," he said, "how do you ever know if you're sunburned? You look well-done all the time!"

Lily and Reni had to hold *each other* back by then. Lily knew it was time to get to work at that day's meeting.

First, she taught them all how to stand and how to walk, which was hard inside the tiny playhouse. She also taught them how to come into a room and introduce themselves. Reni picked it all up right away. But Zooey couldn't seem to keep her mouth from hanging open and saying, "Wow," and Suzy couldn't quite bring herself to look anybody in the eye. After three sessions, they weren't showing a lot of improvement, but Lily moved on to hair and lip gloss so they wouldn't lose interest.

Suzy's thick, straight dark hair didn't want to do anything except fall silkily against her cheeks the way it always did, but when Lily put some almost-pink gloss on her lips and Suzy saw herself in the mirror, she smiled.

"Suzy, that looks good on you, girl!" Reni said.

Lily studied Suzy's face critically. She didn't think the little bit of shine on Suzy's lips made that much difference, but she did look prettier somehow.

"Hey," Zooey said. "She smiled!"

"So?" Reni shrugged. She sometimes had trouble following rule number four when it came to Zooey.

"She hardly ever smiles," Zooey said. "You look good smiling, Suzy!"

Suzy, of course, looked down at her shoes.

When it was Zooey's turn, it wasn't as easy to find her best features and highlight them the way Lily was learning to do. Lily sure wished Kathleen could help. But since the modeling school was still a secret to everyone except Reni, Lily had to do the best she could on her own.

Zooey's hair was thin and the color of wheat bread, and Lily was sure somebody had given her a haircut with a lawn mower. They all wished for a curling iron, but nobody had one her mom would let her take out of the house. Zooey was almost in tears until Lily remembered something Kathleen had said in class to a girl who had a round face and baby cheeks. She'd said to pull her hair up to make it look . . . Well, Lily couldn't remember that part, but a hair tie was found, and Lily pulled some of Zooey's hair up into it on top of her head, and Reni brushed the rest of it until it was shiny. Suzy, who was the only one with bangs, took some gel and created some bangs over Zooey's forehead. Lily wasn't sure it was an improvement, but Zooey was glowing before she even looked in the mirror.

"You guys are nice to me," she said.

"We gotta be," Reni said. "The rules say so. Now be still or this lip gloss'll go up your nose for sure."

Zooey had full lips like Lily's, only her mouth was small like a little bow. They looked cute with some shine on them. She looked like a cherub. Who'd have thought?

"Definitely blush," Reni said as she surveyed the finished Zooey. "Ya'll white girls got the palest skin."

"I'm sorry," Zooey almost whispered.

"What for? You're supposed to be white. Now hold *still!*"

Lily was about to remind Reni about rule number four again, but Zooey's feelings obviously weren't hurt. She was beaming so brightly, she really didn't need any blush. And when Zooey looked in the mirror, Lily was sure she was going to split right open in delight.

"Look at me!" she said.

"You look good," Suzy said shyly.

"You look great!" Lily looked around at them. "We all do. Let's walk like we know we look good!"

Lily was sure if Shad Shifferdecker had seen them, he probably would have folded in half laughing. But the four girls were grinning all the way into their eyes, even Suzy. Lily tossed her hair in the breeze and imagined a filmy skirt blowing out behind her. Next session, maybe they'd talk about clothes.

✿

The next day at school, when the collages all went up around the room and each person had to tell the class about his or hers, Lily hoped they could all get those smiles back. She decided it was kind of like a test.

Ms. Gooch called on Reni first. When she went up to the bulletin board, Lily squeezed her hand and Zooey whispered, "Good luck." Even Suzy took her eyes off her desktop to show her support. Getting up in front of the class was something everybody hated—except Shad, who didn't care what he had to do as long as it got him some attention.

"I did my vision on what I want to do when I'm all done with school and everything," Reni said, jabbing her finger at her collage. "Only I can't decide what I want to do, so I put a whole bunch of stuff on there."

Shad sighed loudly. Ms. Gooch looked hard at him, but she didn't say anything.

"I put, like, horse trainer," Reni went on as she continued to point to the collage. "Veterarian—"

"Veter-in-arian," Marcie called out.

Ms. Gooch cocked an eyebrow.

"Um, dog breeder, dolphin trainer, like the person that uses dolphins to help, like, crippled kids and stuff—"

Shad snored loudly. When Lily looked up, he was dropping his head onto Ashley's shoulder. Ashley pulled away, but she was laughing.

"All right, people," Ms. Gooch said. "That's enough."

It sure is, Lily thought. She looked anxiously at Reni, who was now just jabbing her finger at pictures and shrugging a lot.

"Go ahead, Reni," Ms. Gooch told her. "We're listening."

No, they're not. Lily shifted in her seat and tried to catch Reni's eye to nod at her. Reni turned from her collage and looked right at Lily. And then she seemed to remember something. She straightened her shoulders and let her arms fall to her sides, and she looked Ms. Gooch right in the eye.

"I'm done," she said. And then she went to her desk.

"Let's give Reni a round of applause!" Ms. Gooch said.

Lily, bursting with pride for Reni, clapped enthusiastically. The rest of the class offered a halfhearted spattering of applause.

That's all right, Reni, Lily wanted to whisper to her.

But Zooey evidently didn't agree. Her hand shot up into the air, and before Ms. Gooch could call on her, she said, "I think you should have a rule."

Ms. Gooch lifted an eyebrow. "I have lots of rules, Zooey. You want me to add another one?"

"No, dude!" Shad said.

Now *he wakes up*, Lily thought. She rolled her eyes at Reni.

"Yes." Zooey lifted up her chin. "You oughta have a rule that people in here aren't allowed to say things that make other people feel . . . um . . ." She stopped, her face going red, and turned around in her chair. "How does that one rule go, Lily?"

Lily stared at her. She saw Reni give Zooey a poke and out of the corner of her eye watched Suzy park her face firmly into her folded arms on the desk.

Ms. Gooch laughed. "Do you have your own set of rules, Lily?"

"No!" Lily shook her head and looked hard at Zooey. Something dawned in Zooey's eyes, and she clapped her hand over her mouth.

"What was *that* all about?" Ashley asked.

"She's so weird," Chelsea said.

"You see what I mean?" Zooey's face was red all the way up to her new bangs. "People get to say whatever they want, and that's not right. It—" She turned again to Lily, the right answer glowing in her eyes. "It hurts people's feelings. That's it!"

"'It hurts people's feelings,'" Shad said in a whiny, mocking voice that came out through his nose. "Poor baby!"

Ms. Gooch snapped her fingers at him, and then she looked at the class.

"What do you think, people? Should we make a rule that we can't say things to hurt people's feelings? Let's discuss this."

Hands shot up all over the room. Everybody had a comment.

"I don't think that many people are being mean," Marcie said without being called on. "I just think it's that some other people get their feelings hurt too easy."

"And some people just blurt out whatever they want, whenever they want," Ashley said. She looked right at Marcie. Marcie stuck out her tongue. Ms. Gooch gave them a finger-snapping *and* an eyebrow.

Lily pulled a piece of paper out of her notebook and grabbed her favorite purple-inked pen.

Reni, Zooey, and Suzy, she wrote. *Even if she makes*

it a rule, Shad will never follow it. Let's stick to our plan. P.T.O.

P.T.O. meant Pass This On, and Reni did, first to Zooey, who passed it to Suzy. Nobody else noticed because they were all in a lively discussion about rules and punishments and what was fair and what wasn't.

All except Shad. He yawned elaborately before looking at Lily and crossing his little eyes at her. She just looked back at him. Then he pulled Leo over to him by the shirtsleeve and whispered in his ear while staring at Lily.

Yeah. He was going to be hard to change. Somehow, she *had* to get him to that modeling show.

Eight

hat very night, Kathleen came to class with a stack of white envelopes and a brighter-than-usual smile.

"It's getting close," she said, her perfect eyes twinkling.

Lily put aside her usual attempt to get her eyes to look like that and gazed curiously at the stack of envelopes. She was dying to know what they were, but this wasn't like Ms. Gooch's class. Nobody shouted out stuff or raised their hands to ask a bunch of questions Kathleen would answer anyway if anybody gave her the chance.

We're getting so poised, Lily thought. She crossed her ankles just so and tried to look expectant. Beside her, Cassie was clicking her polished Midnight Mauve fingernails together.

"These," Kathleen said when she was finished teasing them with her silence, "are your invitations to the modeling show we're going to give in just two weeks."

There was a ripple of excitement. Cassie's fingernails clicked louder.

"I have exactly ten for each of you—one for each *person* you would like to invite, not each *family*."

Lily's head turned immediately into a calculator. Mom, Dad, Joe, Art—that was four. Reni, Zooey, Suzy—that made seven. Plus somebody to bring them, maybe Mrs. Johnson—that made eight.

She gave a long sigh of relief. That left two—one for Shad and one for somebody to bring *him*.

"You will notice," Kathleen was saying as she doled out the envelopes in little piles of ten, "that our event will be held on a Thursday evening at 7:00 p.m. at the Riverside Garden Club. The space is limited, which is why you may invite only ten people." She stopped and gave them all a sly look. "There are several important people *I* am going to invite, of course."

Cassie could no longer contain herself. Her hand shot up into the air, grazing Lily's arm with a nail as it went.

"Yes, Cassie. Question?"

"Are those important people, like, talent scouts or something? My mom will want to know."

My mom won't, Lily thought suddenly. There was still the question of whether she and Dad were going to let Lily sign on with the Rutledge Agency at the end of the course. It depended on—

Lily felt a sharp pang, a lot like the kind she got when she forgot to do a homework assignment, only worse.

It depended on whether she could find God anywhere in this modeling business, and so far, she hadn't tried very hard.

I'm going to try right now, tonight, she told herself firmly. *I'm going to focus on looking for God. I know He's got to be in this somewhere.*

But that promise faded the minute Kathleen put her stack of ten invitations into Lily's hand. They even *felt* elegant, just lying there on her palm. And then when Lily opened one, she gasped out loud. They were *printed* invitations, done in important-looking black script like someone's perfect handwriting, only it wasn't. Lily ran her fingers reverently across the letters and thought of Shad Shifferdecker being too impressed to say *anything*, much less something insulting and evil. There would only be the disbelieving eyes, the glinting braces as his mouth hung open . . .

In fact, that was *all* she could think of for the rest of the evening. She didn't even show Mom the invitations on the way home. She was determined that Shad was going to be the first one to lay eyes on them. Every time she felt the envelope in the pocket of her skirt the next day at school, she grinned to herself over just how delicious it was going to be.

Once Shad caught her smiling into space between words on the spelling test and whispered across the aisle, "What's the matter, Snobbins? Bad gas?"

She kept smiling and waited for the perfect moment.

It came just before lunch. Everyone else was finishing up a math test, and Lily and Shad were the only ones done—Lily, because math was easy for her; Shad, because he didn't know how to do half the problems and wasn't interested in trying. Ms. Gooch tapped each of them on the shoulder and beckoned them to follow her.

"I have a job for you two," she whispered when they got to her little glass-walled office cubicle.

"I don't have to touch her to do it, do I?" Shad said. He writhed away from Lily as if she had leprosy.

"No, Shad," Ms. Gooch answered patiently.

Lily just patted the envelope in her pocket and tried to let her eyes sparkle the way Kathleen's did.

"You're too weird," Shad whispered.

"I need for you two to count how many books are in each of these stacks and record the number in this notebook." Ms. Gooch pointed to six tottering stacks of beat-up textbooks.

"Where'd all these come from?" Shad asked. "We don't gotta use all these, do we? Dude, they look *old*!"

He has absolutely no poise, Lily thought smugly.

"Don't worry about it," Ms. Gooch said. "I'm putting them all in storage because they're cluttering up the classroom and I'm never going to use them."

"Yeah, but how come—"

"You don't need that much information," Ms. Gooch said. "Just count them. Unless, of course, you want me to give you your next math assignment."

"One, two, three—"

"I thought so." Ms. Gooch gave Lily a knowing smile. "Bring me the list when you're finished, okay?"

"Of course," Lily said, and she kept eye contact with Ms. Gooch until she was all the way out of the room.

"Why do you act like the lady at the bank?" Shad asked Lily when Ms. Gooch was gone.

"What?"

Shad stiffened his neck and pursed his lips. "'Of course, Ms. Gooch,'" he said in a high-pitched voice. "That's the way the lady at the bank talks to my mother, like she's all kissing up to her or somethin'."

Lily could barely keep from laughing out loud. This was too perfect.

"It's called poise," she said. "You should learn about it."

"It's sissy."

"No, it isn't." Lily stifled a meet-in-the-back grin. "Boys can have poise."

"Yeah, right."

"You could see for yourself."

It was time. Lily slid her hand into her pocket and pulled out the envelope, still perfect and unwrinkled. She held it out to him.

"Read this," she said.

Shad looked at it the way he looked at every paper Ms. Gooch had ever passed out and said, "What's *this*?"

"Open it and find out," Lily told him. "It's for you."

Shad gave it one more long, beady-eyed look before he snatched it out of her hand and tore into it. Lily tried not to cringe as the perfect white paper suffered a ruthless rip. She kept her eyes on him as he pulled out the printed card and read, his lips moving soundlessly. It took him so long to read the whole thing, Lily nearly yanked it out of his hand and read it out loud *to* him. But, no—she wanted to enjoy this.

When Shad got to the bottom of the card, he turned it over and looked at the blank side. Then he curled his lip up at Lily. "So?"

"So, there will be boys in it, and you can come. That's an invitation. I—*they*—are only giving out so many, and you can't get in without an invitation."

"Yeah, but why would I want to? Who wants to go to some dumb *fashion* show? It sounds lame!"

Then he crooked his finger and with it flicked the invitation right into Lily's face.

It isn't the fashion show that's lame, Lily thought as she picked the envelope off the floor, jaw tightened, and tenderly tucked the invitation back into her pocket. *I'm the one who's lame. Why did I ever think he would come to it just because I gave him the invitation? There's got to be some other way to get him there.*

She would have loved to ask the Girlz if they had any ideas at that afternoon's meeting, but she hadn't even told Reni about the show yet, and the other two still didn't even know she was going to Rutledge. No, everything had to be just perfect before she told them.

But Lily did have to tell her family. The wipe-off calendar on the refrigerator was already covered with stuff everybody had to do in November. If she didn't get the show on there, it might get crowded out by some faculty party or some dumb soccer practice. Now, talk about lame.

After they all had raised their heads from the blessing at the dinner table that night, she said, "We got our invitations." She'd been holding it back for so long, her voice sounded breathless, even to her. "Kathleen gave them to us last night."

"Invitations to what?" Joe said.

"Why do you sound like you have asthma?" Art said.

It was as bad as Ms. Gooch's class with all the questions. Even Dad had one.

"Who's Kathleen?" he said.

"Another birthday party?" Mom groaned. "I think every person you know has at least two birthdays a year."

Joe let out a shrill whistle. "Yeah!" he said. "Can I do that? Like, have one every six months?"

"Do *not* whistle like that in this house," Mom said. "You're going to pop somebody's eardrum. And then I'm going to pop *you*."

"No!" Lily's poise was slipping away. "Kathleen—at the Rutledge Agency. She gave us our invitations to the modeling show we're giving at the end of the class."

"Why do you need an invitation if you're in it?" Joe said.

"They're not for me. They're for you."

"Lil, hon, your face is getting blotchy," Mom said. "Calm down."

"For *me*?" Joe said, looking like he'd just been offered Brussels sprouts. "What do I want with an invitation to a modeling show? La-ame!"

Lily looked hard at her little brother to make sure he hadn't suddenly been replaced by Shad Shifferdecker.

"*Everyone* calm down," Mom said. "There is no need to get hysterical. Lil, when is it?"

Lily whipped a fresh invitation out of her pocket and handed it to her mother with a flourish across the bowl of green beans. Art tried to snatch it, but Mom was too quick for him. For once, Lily was glad her mother was an athlete.

"Riverside Garden Club." Mom whistled low. "Ritzy."

"Now I *know* I'm not goin'," Joe said.

"Well, where do you expect them to hold it, Gold's Gym?" Art said.

Dad looked up from the iPhone he was consulting and blinked at Art. "They're having the modeling show at the gym?" he asked.

"Uh-oh," Mom said.

That was never a good sound coming out of Mom. Lily felt her heart starting to race. "What uh-oh?" she said.

"Thursday the twenty-eighth. That's right at the start of the state championship tournament."

"Your team goin'?" Joe asked.

"Of course they're going," Art answered for her.

"She'll have them all expelled from school if they don't get to State."

"You exaggerate," Mom said.

"Do not. I've seen you work those chicks. Somebody misses a serve and everybody has to drop for push-ups. I'm surprised you don't carry a whip—"

"Stop. Everybody!" Lily had her hands over her ears, and she knew her eyes were piercing into all of them one by one. There wasn't an ounce of poise in sight.

"She's freakin' out," Art said.

"Art, hush," Dad put his phone down on the place mat and looked at Lily. "You've got our attention," he said.

Lily drilled her eyes into her mom. "Are you saying you can't come to my show?"

"I'm saying it could be a problem if my team makes it—"

"They will," Art put in.

"I have games on Thursday night. I have to be there, Lil. You know that."

Lily looked desperately around the table. "What about everybody else?"

"Hmm. Let's see." Art put one finger up to his mouth as if he were giving it serious thought. "Watch high school girls play volleyball, or watch a bunch of middle school girls pretend they're models. Uh, tough choice." He smirked and then drained the milk from his glass.

"I don't gotta go, do I, Dad?" Joe said.

But Dad ignored him and put his hand on Lily's arm. "You can count on me, Lilliputian," he said. "I wouldn't miss it."

"You will miss it if you don't put it on your calendar," Mom told him, nodding toward his phone.

And then Art launched into a story about a kid in jazz band that day who had choked on a reed, and Lily sulked and let her meat loaf get cold.

I don't care, she told herself. *I'm going to show Shad Shifferdecker—and save all us girls from him and his evil friends. That's all I really care about anyway.*

But at the next class at Rutledge, she very quickly had to care about something else—or there wasn't going to be a modeling show at all.

Nine

Kathleen was late joining them in the classroom, which immediately got the warning butterflies going in Lily's stomach. Kathleen was always on time, just the way she expected them to be.

And when she did hurry in, there was a clump of blondish hair sticking straight out from behind her ear, and her lipstick had worn off. Something was definitely wrong.

"She looks weird tonight," Cassie whispered to Lily.

"Stressed out," said Stinky from the other side.

"She better not be too stressed," Cassie said. "We're supposed to pick out our outfits tonight. Don't tell me she couldn't get the clothes!"

But several racks of inviting-looking garments beckoned from over in the corner, so that wasn't it. Lily was glad when Kathleen raised her hand and everybody got quiet. She was afraid to breathe.

"I may have some bad news for you," Kathleen said. "There's been a mix-up with the Riverside Garden Club. They've scheduled two events on the same night, and one of them is ours. We've been bumped."

"No fair!" one of the boys said. Nobody was thinking about Kathleen's rules at this point.

"No, it isn't," said Kathleen, "but then, life seldom is." Her mouth was in a straight line.

Cassie nodded and whispered to Lily, "She's stressed out all right. I've seen my mother look like that a thousand times."

But Lily was leaning forward in her seat, heart pounding. What was going to happen? Did this mean they weren't going to have their show?

"I don't want anybody panicking," Kathleen was saying. "We will have our show, but we may have to postpone it until I can find a place big enough."

"What about the armory?"

"You could have it at that one movie theater. That's way big!"

"Gold's Gym," Lily muttered.

Kathleen put her hand up again. "I do have one lead, but it would mean having it on Saturday afternoon instead of Thursday night."

For once Lily *wanted* to shout out, and she wanted to shout, "No! Not a Saturday! Shad Shifferdecker hangs out at the mall on Saturdays!" She was about to yell, "Let's have it at the mall!" when Kathleen put her hand up yet again and added a finger snap. Lily bit her lip.

"We might be able to get the middle school at the Cedar Hills school complex, but it would help if someone in our group went to one of the schools there. I know one of you does. Who is that?"

She frowned over the group, and every neck craned.

But I don't want to do it at Cedar Hills! Lily thought. *There's no way I'll ever get Shad near a school on a Saturday!*

"This could be our only option on such short notice," Kathleen said.

"Come on. Raise your hand!" one of the boys said. "What's the big deal?"

It is a big deal—for me, Lily thought. *There has to be some other way.*

And then she saw Kathleen pawing through a stack of files on the table. *Their* files. In about a minute she was going to discover who went to Cedar Hills, and she was going to be disappointed in Lily for not raising her hand.

That would be worse than not having Shad there. Lily shot up her hand and even waved it a little.

"Kathleen!" Cassie said. "It's Lily!"

Kathleen's face broke into the first smile of the evening. "Of course. I remember now. You were the only one I invited from Cedar Hills." She rested her chin on the tips of her fingers. "Will you help us, Lily? May I use your name when I call them back tomorrow?"

It felt like the whole room was holding its breath. Lily let hers out and said, "Sure. My mother works in that complex too. She teaches at the high school."

"Excellent," Kathleen said. Her eyes were shiny again. "Then let's get to choosing our outfits, shall we? And at the end of the evening, I have a surprise for you."

Lily had to admit that she had fun trying on great new clothes to her heart's content. When she and her mother went shopping, Mom would get bored with the whole thing after two try-ons and would say things like, "If you like that one, just get it in three or four colors and let's go home."

After at least a *dozen* try-ons, Lily chose a green-shorts-and-summer-top outfit for her casual wear and topped it off with a cool hat and a pair of sandals with a fun bag to sling over her shoulder. For dressy, she picked a blue sundress with a short denim jacket and shoes that made her walk even taller. The best part, though, was when Kathleen told her she'd made good choices.

"You don't look like the same girl who tried to back out of my office with gum on her skirt." Kathleen eyes twinkled at her. "I think she's disappeared entirely."

Lily wasn't so sure about that, until she saw the surprise: their pictures and their composition cards. The face that smiled out at Lily from a filmy halo of red-gold hair was somebody Lily would have looked at from far away and thought, *I wish I could look like her.*

"I don't think your parents will have any hesitation about letting you sign on with us when they see this," Kathleen said. "And after they see you in the modeling show, they're going to realize that you're a natural. I know it."

She gave Lily's hand a squeeze and moved on to tell one of the boys that he could *not* rip up the jeans he'd picked for the show, but Lily could feel herself slowly deflating like an inner tube going flat. *Mom and Dad aren't going to let me do it if I can't find God in it, and I know that,* she thought. *Tonight? Tonight I'm going to pray and pray and pray and tell God I'm sorry I've been ignoring Him, and it'll be all right.*

She did, the minute she'd said good night to Mom, hugged Dad for the final tuck-in, and the lights were out. She didn't grab for the flashlight and an issue of *Seventeen* the way she usually did at that point. She turned over on her stomach and squeezed her eyes shut and prayed, as Art would have put it, "like a mad dog."

God, I'm sorry I've been so rude to You. I'm as bad as Shad Shifferdecker. No, worse, because he probably doesn't even know any better, but I do. I know how much You love me and want me to figure out who You made me to be, and that's why I know You're in the modeling agency somewhere. Will You please help me find You so I can stay there?

Lily opened her eyes a slit as a thought hit her: What if God didn't want her to stay there? What if, like Mom and Dad said, she wasn't serving Him there? Didn't that make her just as, well, *selfish* as Shad?

But if Shad comes to the show, he'll see that I'm not some bony giraffe with fleas. Then he'll act better, and I'll be the one who did it, which means I've served.

It sounded so good that Lily almost bounded out of bed to go down and tell Mom and Dad right then. But it would be so much better to tell them *after* Shad had eaten every one of his evil words with a fork—no, make that a shovel. Lily fell asleep with a vision of Shad chowing down on words he'd shoved into his mouth with a bulldozer.

But from the moment she got up the next morning, nothing—*absolutely nothing*—went in the right direction.

"I have a game right after school today," Mom said as she crammed sandwiches into the brown bags lined up on the counter. "If we win, we go to State."

"Will you have games next Saturday if you do?" Lily said.

"If we get that far in the tournament."

"You know you're gonna walk all over everybody," Art said. "Hey, since State's gonna be at Cedar Hills, pep band is playing for it."

"So you have to be there too?" Lily said.

Art rolled his eyes at her. "Am I in the pep band?"

"Yeah, but—"

"No, Lily, I *am* the pep band."

"We really need to work with Art on his self-esteem," Dad said dryly as he passed through the kitchen. "Has anybody seen my glasses?"

Joe looked up from the homework he was still finishing at the kitchen table and lowered his eyebrows. "I wish I was in the pep band. No, I wish I was on the team—the water boy, anything! Man, I don't *want* to go to some fashion show!"

"Nobody's asking you to!" Lily said. "I wouldn't want you there if you paid me to let you."

"Huh?" Joe said.

"Lily. Blotchy," Mom said. "And, Joe, don't get your boxers in a bunch, okay, pal? You don't have to go to the fashion show. You'd actually have to comb your hair, and we all know that isn't going to happen."

"It's not a fashion show," Lily said. "It's a modeling show."

"For wannabe models," Art said. "Which one's my lunch, Mom?"

"I hope it's the one with the arsenic in it," Lily said, and she snatched up her backpack and stormed out the back door.

"Does this mean I don't have to walk with her today?" she heard Joe say as the screen door slammed. "She's always telling me to hold my shoulders straight and walk like I look good . . ."

Lily was glad she didn't hear the rest. In fact, all she *could* hear were her own thoughts: *It doesn't matter. I just have to get Shad there. I just have to get Shad there.*

But about the middle of the morning, when they

were just getting into the geography lesson, Lily got a note from the office that erased even that hope.

It was from Kathleen:

Good news, Lily! We have the Cedar Hills Middle School auditorium for our show next Saturday afternoon, thanks to you and your mother! I called her this morning, and she was a great help. I wanted you to be the first to know. I'll see you for our last rehearsal Tuesday.

Kathleen

Lily didn't take the time to notice how perfect Kathleen's handwriting was or even to try to imitate it on her geography worksheet.

She just crumpled the note into a ball and dropped it into the trash can when she went to the pencil sharpener.

She was on her way back to her seat when she felt someone tug at the bottom of her sweater. She thought it was probably Shad, and she was about to abandon poise and snatch it away from him, but when she looked down, she saw it was Kresha Ragina looking shyly back up at her from beneath her tumble of hair.

"No trouble?" she whispered to Lily.

"What?" Lily whispered back.

"Trouble . . . from de office?"

She pointed to the trash can. Lily shook her head.

"No trouble," she answered. "It was just a note from somebody."

Kresha's face lit up like a little sun. "Oh, that's good," she said. "You always so happy, you know? I see you sad, I think, *Oh no. Lee-lee has trouble.* But no?"

"No," Lily told her again.

"Good." Kresha went happily back to trying to decipher her geography book.

Lily felt funny when she got back to her desk. *Kresha notices whether I'm happy or sad? I almost forget about her most of the time.* She watched the Croatian girl now as she sighed heavily and rubbed out something with her eraser. From where Lily sat, it looked as if she'd rubbed several holes in her paper already. Lily felt that I-haven't-done-my-homework pang again.

The only good thing that happened that day was that both Suzy and Zooey were absent. That wasn't such a good thing all by itself, but it meant that Lily and Reni were alone outside during break, and Lily could give her the invitations for the Girlz Only Group. She had neatly crossed out the place and time and written in the new information in the same script as it had been printed in before. Well, almost. Reni was impressed anyway. Lily was glad *somebody* was, and it made her feel a little better.

"I want this to be a surprise for Zooey and Suzy," Lily said. "You can't tell them I'm in it."

"They're going to wonder why you aren't going with us," Reni said. "They barely breathe anymore unless you tell them to."

"Nuh-uh," Lily said. But she kind of liked that idea.

"I could tell them you couldn't go," Reni said, "and I didn't want you to feel bad so I didn't even tell you."

"That would be a lie." Lily thought about her prayer last night and congratulated herself.

"I got it!" Reni's dimples went way deep. "I'll tell

them you're going to meet us there. That's true!"

"Yeah! You just don't have to tell them *how* I'm going to meet you."

"This is gonna be totally cool," Reni said.

Lily was almost convinced that it was. She felt so much better, in fact, that when she practiced her pivots in the living room again that night, she ignored Art and Joe's imitations of her, the ones that made them look like bewildered ostriches. She even started to think that maybe getting Shad to the show wasn't a lost cause yet. She still had a week to think of something.

Ten

Mom's team won their game that afternoon. They were going to State for sure. Everybody in the family was thrilled about it except Lily. Every evening that week, Mom had her team in special practices.

"I told you she works those chicks like dogs," Art said on Tuesday. "Get out the whip. She'll be wanting to use it before the week's over."

But Mom wasn't the only one cracking some kind of instrument of torture. The band teacher had the pep band in special rehearsals twice that week so they'd be ready to wow everybody at the tournament starting Thursday, just two days before the modeling show. Art might "*be* the pep band," but he too had to go to practice.

That meant it was Lily, Dad, and Joe for supper most nights that week, and on Thursday, when the tournament finally started, Joe went to his friend Ryan's house to eat before the game because he said he was sick of Dad's cooking.

Lily was getting a little tired of macaroni and cheese from a box herself, but she was too loyal to Dad to bail out and go to Reni's. In fact, she decided she and Dad could come up with something better.

"You've always loved mac and cheese," Dad said.

"That was when I was *young*," Lily said. "My tastes have matured."

"Oh." Dad looked a little confused. "The only other thing I know how to make is bacon and eggs."

"Yeah!" Lily said. "And I'll make some toast and set the table. I think we should have flowers for a centerpiece."

So Dad poked around in the refrigerator and miraculously found all the ingredients while Lily dug into the back of the cabinet for some real dishes. During volleyball tournaments, Mom always used paper plates. She said it saved her sanity.

The bacon was curling and bubbling in the frying pan, the eggs were waiting patiently in a bowl to be scrambled, and the table looked like the cover of *Martha Stewart Living*, as far as Lily was concerned, when the phone rang. Dad answered it and began a too-long conversation.

"I'm going to have to look that up for you," Lily heard Dad say as she refolded the napkins for the third time. "Can you hold on?"

He set the phone on the table and said to Lily, "Watch that bacon, would you? I have to go find . . . have you seen my glasses?"

He went off to his study, still muttering, and Lily finished fiddling with the napkins. Then she gave the eggs a stir in their bowl. The bacon didn't look all brown and hard yet the way Dad liked it, so she just poked at it a little with a fork.

The bread was already toasted and buttered and keeping warm in the oven, and she'd put five kinds of jelly on the table. There was nothing else to do but perch on the stool and think about the show—and Shad Shifferdecker.

Lily still hadn't come up with a way to get him there, and the show was going to be *so good*. Just the night before, at their dress rehearsal, Kathleen had privately announced that Lily would start the show—that she would be the first one out on the runway!

"You'll get the audience's attention," she'd said. "They'll know right away that this isn't a kiddie show. This is professional, the real thing."

It was just one more reason why Shad had to be there. She was so anxious to have him in that audience, she'd even asked him that afternoon at school, "Shad, do you really go to the mall and hang out every Saturday?"

He'd looked at her for a second with his mouth kind of half hanging open. "Yeah," he finally answered. "Why do you want to know?"

"Just curious." That was only half true, but she couldn't get herself to say, "Just *desperate!*"

"Mostly we hang around the food court till they kick us out. Then we go to the video game place till they kick us outta there. Then we try to sneak into Abercrombie, but if they catch a kid in there without parents, they, like, hold you and call the security guard or something."

"Did that ever happen to you?" Lily asked.

"Nah," Shad said. "I'm too good for 'em. I, like, 'blend in.'" He got a sly look on his face. "You'd never make it with that hair. They'd spot you like that." He snapped his fingers right under Lily's nose.

She hadn't known where to go from there, so she'd just looked at him.

"There you go again, givin' me that creepy look," Shad said. "You freak me out."

Lily took in a deep breath to sigh now, but she

stopped in mid-sniff. Something didn't smell like it was supposed to.

She glanced at the stove, and she could feel her eyes popping. The frying pan was smoking like a chimney. One look told her that the bacon was dry and hard *now*.

She grabbed for a pot holder and started to lift the pan off the burner. But there were flames starting to lick at the grease in the bottom.

"Dad!" Lily yelled. "The bacon's burning!"

There was no answer from the study, and the flame tongues were lashing up higher. Heart racing, Lily dove for the sink and snatched up the first thing her hand hit—the empty iced tea pitcher. Still screaming for her father, she filled up the pitcher and made another dive for the stove.

By now the flames were reaching up for the hood over the stove top. Lily held on to the pitcher with both hands and flung its contents into the pan.

Suddenly all she saw was a flash of gold as the fire rushed at her like a genie coming out of a bottle. Something bit, hard and hot, at her face, and she dropped the pitcher and started to fling her hands at her cheeks. Hands caught her from behind and pulled her back.

"Don't touch it!" Dad cried.

"I didn't touch it!"

But Dad wasn't talking about the blazing frying pan. He was talking about Lily's face. He brought both of his palms against her cheeks and slapped at them until Lily was screaming. Then he put something wet and cold over her whole face.

"Hold that there!" he shouted.

He *had* to shout. There was so much noise in the

kitchen now—the fire crackling and the bacon grease popping like gunshots and the smoke detector screaming—that Lily could barely hear her own thoughts.

But then she did hear a shriek that made her tear the wet towel from her face in terror. Dad clutched one hand under his opposite armpit while he beat back the flames with a wet towel held in the other. Through the smoke Lily could see his face twisted like a Halloween mask.

"Can you get the fire extinguisher?" Dad shouted to her.

Lily dropped her own wet towel and yanked the extinguisher off the wall. She held it out to Dad, but he shook his head. "You'll have to do it!" he shouted.

He was coughing now, and so was Lily. In fact, she wasn't sure she could even breathe anymore. Hacking from her throat and squinting her eyes, she managed to push the right button. Foam leaped from the little hose and tried to smother the flames, but they fought back stubbornly.

"Come on!" Dad cried. "Let's get outside!"

Lily was still squirting as Dad hooked his arm around her elbow and hauled her out the back door. It was only when they'd stumbled down the back steps and he let go of her that Lily saw that his hands were white and charred-looking.

"Daddy, you're burned!"

"I know, sweetheart. Come on. Let's get to a phone!"

But someone obviously already had, for just then there was a high-pitched wail from down the street, and the early-evening dark was shot through with red lights. Crooking his arm through Lily's again, Dad pulled her to the front yard.

"Daddy, you're hurt bad!" Lily cried. "You can't even use your hands!"

"It's all right. I'm fine!"

When they got to the front yard, however, and ran straight into the front of a big man in an even bigger black coat, it turned out Dad wasn't fine at all.

"Ambulance is on its way!" the man shouted over the din of sirens and shouting and water-shooting. "Lie down out here, out of the smoke!"

Two other men in heavy coats ushered Lily and her father across the street to a spot on the sidewalk where someone else had already spread blankets. They made Dad lie on one, and Lily squatted down beside him. But one of the men took Lily gently by the shoulder and pushed her onto the other.

"My dad is hurt!" Lily cried.

"So are you, hon," said the fireman. "I can hear the ambulance coming. They'll take good care of both of you. Just lie still now."

"I'm not hurt!" Lily wailed. "It's my dad who's hurt!"

But when two ambulances had screamed to a halt and a woman in a blue shirt leaned over her, Lily saw the look in her eyes, and she knew she was wrong. She *was* hurt. Why else would Miss Blue Shirt be barking out orders to someone behind her and taking Lily's pulse and telling her everything was going to be all right when her eyes were sparking out that it most definitely wasn't?

"What hospital do you want to go to, sir?" someone asked.

"Baptist Medical Center," someone said in a frail voice.

Why isn't Dad answering? Lily thought. *What happened?*

"Daddy?" she called out. Her own voice sounded whistle-shrill.

"I'm right here, Lilliputian," said that same weak voice.

"What's your name, sweetie?" asked Miss Blue Shirt.

"Lilianna. What about my dad?"

"Your dad's going to the hospital, and so are you. My name's Patti, and I'll be taking care of you."

"I want to go with my dad."

"He's going to need a lot of room in his ambulance, Lilianna. You and I will have our own private ride. How's that?"

"Is he all right?"

"I'm all right, Lilliputian. You just do what they say. I'll see you there."

Lily lifted her head to watch them lift Dad onto a gurney, but Patti put something over her nose and gently pushed Lily's head back.

"You'll get one of those too," Patti said. "Why don't you just relax and let me do all the work?"

Lily didn't have much choice. Once she was bundled up and put on a gurney and slid into the back of the ambulance like a casserole going into the oven, there wasn't much she could do—except pray. And that she did, very, very hard.

At first when they got to the hospital, a whole team of people crowded around Lily's gurney as they rolled it into a room with curtains all around. But once Patti had shouted a bunch of numbers at them and several team members inspected her face and asked her if she knew where she was and what her name was, things calmed down. Lily thought crazily that she must have given them the right answers. She wasn't sure how, because her head was spinning.

"You have a couple of burns, Lilianna, okay?" explained a doctor with almost no hair. "We're going to give you something to help you relax, and then we're going to take care of those burns. You'll be fine, okay?"

"What about my dad?"

"I'll send somebody to check on Dad, okay?"

Then she felt a sting in her arm, and before too long her eyes got heavy. Her lips were heavy too when she said to the doctor, "Did you know you end every sentence with *okay*?" After that, she went off into a sleep with no dreams at all.

When Lily woke up, she knew her face was on fire again before she even opened her eyes. She flailed at the blanket and tried to sit up, but a sure, familiar arm stopped her.

"Whoa, girl," Mom said. "You're about to hit the sidewalk running."

"They're burning again, Mom!" she said.

"What is, Lil?"

"My cheeks!"

There was the smallest of pauses before Mom said, "They're not burning anymore. I know it hurts, but the fire's out."

Mom finally came into focus, and Lily realized she was still in that room with the curtains, except the team of doctors and nurses had left, and there was only Mom. She was in her Cedar Hills High volleyball team sweatshirt, and her face looked as gray as the shirt did.

"Do you remember what happened?" Mom said.

"Dad was cooking bacon, and the grease caught on fire,

and I tried to put it out. Only then there was more fire, and Dad got burned."

"And so did you," Mom said. "Yours are only second degree though. I know it hurts, but you're going to be fine."

Lily put her hands up to her cheeks. All she could feel were bandages that felt two inches thick.

"I'm burned on my face?" she said.

"One on each side." Mom forced a grin. "They match. Leave it to you to do it perfect—"

"What about Daddy? His hands were all burned, Mom!"

Her mother's grin faded. "Your dad wasn't as lucky as you were. He's burned all the way up to his elbows on both arms—some second degree, some third."

"What does that mean, all those degrees?" Lily's heart was pounding, and the tears were already stinging in her eyes.

"It means he's in a lot of pain, and he's going to need some surgery and physical therapy. It's going to be a long haul."

A sob wrenched Lily's face, and that hurt even more, and that made her want to cry even more.

"Ohhh, talk about salt in the wound, Lil," Mom said. "Come on. Try not to cry. Let me get a Kleenex. There you go. Just breathe through it."

"I can't!" Lily said. She tried to shake her head, but that hurt too.

"Daddy's going to be fine," Mom said. "It's going to take time, but he'll pull through. We'll all help him. We have to thank God it wasn't worse."

"It was my fault."

"Don't even go there, Lil. It was no one's fault. If

it was anyone's fault, it was mine for not just order-
ing you two a pizza. Who knew you were going to pick
tonight to try gourmet cooking?" Mom laughed, but she
reminded Lily of Suzy: her laughter was nervous, and it
never reached her eyes.

"I'm sorry," Lily said.

"There's no need to be. It wasn't your fault, and if
you get yourself all upset, you're only going to hurt more.
Come on. Just breathe easy and I'll pray."

"God must hate me. I hardly ever pray anymore—"

"Lilianna." Mom never used *Lilianna* unless she was
really serious. "We're not going to have that kind of talk.
God loves you. Period. End of discussion. Now close your
eyes. Let's talk to Him."

Lily did close her eyes, but all she could see were
flames reaching out and grabbing her, grabbing Dad.

"Mom?" she whispered when the prayer was done.
"Dad *is* gonna be all right, isn't he?"

"Yes. The doctors have all assured me. They wouldn't
lie. I wouldn't lie."

Still, Lily cried. Even though the tears stung as they
trailed down into her bandages, she cried. She cried for
a long time while Mom kept her head bowed.

Eleven

The doctor with almost no hair let Lily go home from the hospital the next morning. While Mom was downstairs signing papers, a nurse came in carrying a helium-filled pink balloon and smiling like she didn't have an off switch.

"You get to go home and be pampered all day, lucky lady." She tied the balloon to the arm of Lily's wheelchair.

"I don't think anybody's going to wait on me," Lily said as she slid into the chair. "We don't pamper at my house."

"Lots of ice cream and DVDs," the nurse continued, as if Lily hadn't even answered. "You can be queen for a day."

She wheeled Lily out into the hall, and Lily was about to say they didn't do "queen" at the Robbins house when she caught sight of her reflection in the shining stainless steel elevator doors. A gasp escaped before she could stop it.

It was the first time she'd seen herself since the fire, and the sight sent a long shudder down her back.

A large bandage covered each side of her face. She knew that—she'd felt them with her hands last night—but she had no idea the rest of her face was bright red and that her forehead was swollen and threatening to tumble down over her eyebrows. She didn't know her eyelids were as puffy as biscuits or that her eyes were the color of Cassie's fingernail polish. She hadn't realized she looked like a freak.

The elevator doors slid open and split the bandaged freak in two.

"So you just snuggle onto the couch when you get home," the nurse was saying, "and drink everything you like to drink, the more liquids the better."

But the only liquids Lily could think about right then were the tears spilling from her eyes.

She was glad that when Mom joined her at the front door of the hospital, she didn't continue the nurse's nonstop grinning. In fact, as she pulled the car away from the curb, she looked as glad to leave the nurse behind as Lily was.

"That woman was far too cheerful," Mom said. "Nobody should be allowed to smile that much this early in the morning."

"I might never smile again."

"Are you hurting? They sent some pain medication home with us."

"I'm a freak now! My forehead looks like it belongs on a baboon!"

"The swelling will go down," Mom said. "You aren't going to be Ape Woman for more than a day."

"Mo-om!"

"Lil—come on. Don't lose your sense of humor. Dad still has his, and he's got a long way to go before he looks human again."

Lily blinked back the newest onslaught of tears. "Are you coming back to get him after you drop me off?"

"Uh, no." Mom stopped at a red light and tilted her head at Lily. Her brown doe-eyes looked suddenly sad. "He isn't going to be home for at least a week," she said. "He's having surgery right now. I have to come back as soon as I get you settled. I'm sorry I didn't make that clear, hon."

As Mom cruised the car forward again, all Lily could do was stare straight ahead. The road disappeared in a blur of tears, and her already burning face flamed even hotter.

What's wrong with me? she thought miserably. *Here I am whining because my face is messed up, and my dad is having some awful operation! I'm a horrible person!*

Lily had never felt shame like this before. It burned into parts of her that hadn't been touched by the kitchen fire. She wanted to shake it out of her, run away, hide her whole horrible self under the mess in the backseat.

But she knew no matter what she did, she couldn't get away from it. The shame burned inside her like a grease fire that couldn't be put out.

"Now remember, he's going to be all right," Mom said. "They have to repair some damage and it's going to be painful for him, but he'll be able to use his hands again just fine. He'll be home, driving us all nuts looking for his glasses before you know it."

Lily flung her face into her hands and burst into fresh tears. They stung her eyes and her face, and the sobs choked up her throat, but she couldn't stop.

"God love you," Mom said. "I know this is torture for you. You've got more feelings than Art and Joe and me all put together."

That only made Lily cry harder. *She thinks I'm all*

good and wonderful because I'm crying for Dad, Lily thought as more sobs broke out of her chest. *But all I am is selfish and vain.* She wrapped her arms around herself as her body started to shake. *You were wrong, Mom*, she wanted to cry out. *God* must *hate me now.*

She was crying so hard that she didn't notice they weren't headed home until they pulled into Reni's driveway.

"I don't want to see anybody, Mom," Lily managed to say.

"You don't have much choice," Mom said. "I have to get back to the hospital. Mrs. Johnson will take good care of you."

"I can take care of myself. Why can't I just go home?"

"Nobody's going home for several days," Mom said. "The smell in there is enough to gag a maggot."

"What smell?" Lily asked.

Mom gave her a teasing almost-grin. "You and your father tried to burn the house down, remember? Nobody's going to live in there until the cleaning service gets the stench out."

"We didn't try to—"

"Would you lighten up, Lil? I'm teasing you. Everything is going to be fine. You kids should love it. Until the kitchen's redone we're going to have to eat out or order in every night."

Lily was certain she'd never eat again even when, after Mom left, Reni's mother offered her pancakes, waffles with strawberries and whipped cream—anything she wanted.

"I'm really not hungry," Lily said. "Can I just go to Reni's room and lie down?"

"Your mama says you have to keep fluids in you at

all times." Mrs. Johnson smiled and showed the same deep dimples Reni had. "So what's your pleasure? Coke? Sprite? Lemonade?"

"Water," Lily said.

"One water coming up."

But the minute Mrs. Johnson put the frosty pitcher and the glass with a curlicue straw on the bedside table and left Reni's room, Lily turned her face to the wall and cried until she fell asleep.

When she woke up, she heard whispering. She was sure someone was saying, "She nearly burned her father up, and all she could think about was her precious face." But as she shook off the ugly cobwebs of her dream, she opened her eyes and saw Kathleen.

She wanted to pull the covers up over her head.

"Hey, there!" Kathleen sank—elegantly, of course—into a chair Mrs. Johnson had pulled up to the bed before she tiptoed out. "You gave us all quite a scare."

"Don't look at me," Lily said, "or you'll really get a scare."

Kathleen surveyed Lily's face and slowly shook her head. "This isn't the *best* look for you," she said, "but if anybody can pull it off, you can."

Lily blinked. "Pull what off?"

"The show. Your mom said the doctor told her it should be no problem for you to walk down a runway a couple of times. We'll have extra help for you for your changes, but—"

"I can't be in the show!" Lily almost shouted. Her voice was scratchy and pitiful, but she didn't care.

"Excuse me?"

"You don't want me in your show! I look like a baboon!"

Kathleen sat back in the chair and folded her hands neatly in her lap so that all her nails lined up in a polished, white-tipped row. She seemed to look at Lily forever, until Lily had to turn her own eyes miserably down to Reni's comforter.

"In the first place," Kathleen finally said, "it isn't 'my' show; it's 'our' show. It's very much all of ours, and I can't imagine it happening without you."

"But—"

"And in the second place, you look absolutely nothing like a primate of any kind. You are a beautiful young woman with some bandages on her face. Yes, your forehead is swollen, but I'm practically watching it go down as I sit here."

Lily shrugged.

"I'm surprised at you," Kathleen said.

"Why?"

"I was convinced that you understood that we're not about drop-dead gorgeous at Rutledge. We're about poise and self-confidence. We're about being healthy and setting a good example for other girls your age who think they have to wear gobs of makeup and labels to be someone."

The comforter began to blur.

"And *you* are the most poised, the most confident, and therefore the most beautiful person in our class."

"I'm not beautiful right now. Look at me."

"Have you been listening?"

"I'm ugly on the inside. I was supposed to look for God in modeling, and I never did. I got so wrapped up in being this show-off and wanting to throw it in Shad Shifferdecker's face, that I—I burned the kitchen and burned my father, and when he was lying in some operating room, all I did was—was whine b-b-because I looked like an ape."

Kathleen probably didn't understand half of that, but she leaned forward, nodding her head as if she'd comprehended every word. She picked up Lily's hand and held it gently between hers. "Bless you, Lily." Her usually very shiny eyes were velvet soft. "There's a battle going on in there, isn't there?"

Lily could only nod and cry. She knew snot must be bubbling at her nostrils, but who cared?

"And do you know who the enemy is?" Kathleen asked.

Lily shook her head.

"It's you."

Lily took the Kleenex Kathleen handed her and swabbed at her eyes, which was pointless since more tears just kept coming out.

"You're being much, much too hard on yourself. Much harder than God is being, I'm sure of that."

"You know about God?" Lily said.

Kathleen gave her air-filled laugh. "I'm a Christian too. If you'd told me you were looking for God at Rutledge, I'd have pointed Him out all over the place! And I would have started right here."

She put a shiny nail to Lily's chest.

"Not in me," Lily said.

"Yes, in you. How on earth do you think you got all that poise?"

"You taught me."

"I taught you to look at the special gifts and qualities *God* gave you." She smiled. "Actually, we shouldn't call it *self*-confidence. We ought to call it *God*-confidence."

"Why would God have confidence in me? All I cared about was showing up Shad Shifferdecker."

"I don't know who in the world Shad Shifferdecker is, but I do know we don't need to worry about how much confidence God has in *us*. I mean, we disappoint Him all the time. It's much more important to put all *our* confidence in *Him*."

"I don't get it."

"Okay, let me ask you this: Do you have confidence that God loves you? That He forgives you for the things you've done that are obviously driving you into a frenzy?"

"I don't know," Lily said. She looked down at the comforter again, but Kathleen reached over and lifted her chin with the tips of her elegant fingers.

"Then we need to pray, my friend."

Suddenly it seemed to grow very still in Reni's room. Kathleen took Lily's hand again, and she sighed, soft and deep, as if she were letting out all her air to make room for God. And then she began to pray.

"Father," she said, "we have one of Your little ones here who has forgotten how much You love her. Will You please reassure her? Will You fill her with Your love and Your forgiveness? Will You help her to see past her shame and her guilt and run to You with open arms again?

"Will You hold her on your lap and let her know that she's beautiful—inside and out—because You made her? Please, kiss away the fear that makes her want to hide under the covers. Bring her out into the light again, Lord, where she can see You everywhere she goes. In the name of Jesus we pray."

Lily didn't hear the "amen." She was crying too hard.

Kathleen stayed until Lily was calmed down enough

to be talked into an orange juice with crushed ice. Before she left, Kathleen said to Lily, "God will show you what to do. You just have to have confidence in Him."

After that, it seemed like no time before Mom was there, wearing the smile she usually reserved for victories in state championships.

"Your dad is doing great," she announced. "The doctor said the operation couldn't have gone better, and Dad'll be able to have visitors tonight. You think you'll be up for it?"

Lily stared down into her second orange juice. It was going to be hard to face Dad, but Kathleen had said God would be there. She looked back at her mother.

"I think so," she said.

Mom's doe-eyes widened. "Well, I'm glad you ran off little Miss Let-Me-Go-Hide-Under-a-Rock." She sighed and took the glass of iced tea Mrs. Johnson handed her.

"You look exhausted," Mrs. Johnson told her. "How on earth are you going to coach another game tonight?"

Lily blinked. "Did you win last night?"

"We did," Mom said. "Even with me gone half the game." Mom took a sip. "It's funny. It just doesn't seem that important to me now. Something like this sure changes your perspective."

Lily wasn't sure what "perspective" was, but she recognized the guilty pang that went through her.

Maybe I shouldn't do the modeling show after all, she thought. *It really isn't that important, like Mom said.*

Mom tapped Lily lightly on the head. "What's going on in there?" she said. "I can almost hear the wheels turning."

"Kathleen says I should still do the show because it's about inside beauty and God-confidence, but it doesn't seem important, like you said."

"Oh, I think it's more important than ever now," Mom said.

Lily felt her puffy-red eyes bulging. "You do?"

"I do. But let's see what your dad says when we talk to him tonight."

Lily swallowed down a big lump. This was going to be hard. She sure hoped God would show up.

He will, she reminded herself. *I have to have confidence.*

Twelve

When Reni came home from school, Lily still had the urge to pull the comforter up over her face again. It hadn't occurred to her until then: Would Reni still want to be seen with Lily—to have her as a best friend—with her face all bandaged up like a mummy's?

But Reni didn't stare or act weird when she came into the room. She went straight to the bed, sat down, and hugged Lily's neck. "Wow. Does it hurt?"

"Yeah, some. I know I look funky."

"What's it look like under the bandages?"

"I don't know."

"When do you get to look?"

Reni was making it sound like an adventure or something. Lily sat up and got interested.

"I guess I could look tomorrow when my mom changes them," she said. "What I think is weird is my forehead."

"It just looks like you have a sunburn. You could cover that up with a head scarf, though. Check it out."

Reni produced a fringy plaid scarf from her drawer and gently wrapped it around Lily's forehead. She fiddled with it for a few minutes, her dimples deep, and then handed Lily a mirror. The overgrown forehead was swathed in color. She looked like one of those girls who could pull off funky stuff like that.

"Wow," Lily said. "That looks good."

"Of course. You're the one who taught us to do the best we can with what we've got."

At the mention of the Girlz, Lily felt her heart sink. Reni frowned.

"What's wrong? I've got other scarves if you hate that one—"

"No . . . It's just, if I do the show, you'd better tell Suzy and Zooey about it before they come—you know, that I'm in it. Don't surprise them."

"How come?"

"Because. What if they'd feel weird sitting there watching somebody walking around on the stage in bandages? If you tell them now, they can, like, back out."

"*I'm* not backing out."

"Yeah, but you're my best friend."

"Suzy and Zooey are your friends too. They think you hung the moon or something."

"They think I did w*hat*?"

"My mom says that. It's like if you told them they should wear garbage bags for dresses, they'd do it."

"Nuh-uh."

"Yuh-huh."

"Not *now*."

Reni just shrugged, and they were quiet for a few minutes while that conversation evaporated.

"So what do you want to do, I mean, right now?" Reni said finally.

"I don't know."

"It seems weird not having a meeting. That's, like, what we do after school."

"We could just talk, I guess," Lily said.

Reni gave her a nudge. "Move over." She crawled in under the comforter beside Lily.

"You know what I'm thinkin'?" she said.

"What?"

"I'm thinkin' if you did the modeling show, you'd be like some girl in a book, bein' all brave goin' out there with bandages on your face."

"I don't feel like a heroine."

"A what?"

"That's a girl in a book."

"What *do* you feel like?"

Lily looked at Reni, and Reni looked back at her. "I'm scared," Lily whispered.

"Yeah," Reni said. "I would be too."

Later that afternoon, Lily and Mom and Art and Joe checked into a suite at the Comfort Inn.

"Live it up, kids," Mom said. "It's only for a week."

Joe made a dive for the TV remote. "Hey, cool! They've got satellite!"

Art checked out the rates for various services posted in a book on the desk and said, "Who's pickin' up the tab for all this?"

"The insurance company," Mom said.

Art looked at Lily. "Lucky for you, you little arsonist. Otherwise, you'd be forking over your allowance for the rest of your life."

"All right! Listen to me, both of you boys." Mom's voice had that sharp edge they hadn't heard since the day Joe had tried to slide a pencil up Lily's nose while she was sleeping. All three of them froze in mid-move and watched her. Mom shoved the sleeves of her sweatshirt up to her elbows and stared them down. Gone were the doe-eyes. She was no-nonsense from eyebrows to cornea. "I have let this go on far too long, and I'm putting a stop to it right now."

"To what?" Art said.

"I think you know exactly what, but let me spell it out for you."

Even Joe had an uh-oh look by now, and Lily's heart was doing double time. The burns on her face suddenly stung harder than ever.

What did I do now? she thought. *God, I'm having a hard time having confidence here.*

Just as Lily felt as if she were about to simply shrivel up and die from the agony of waiting, Mom said, "There will be no more of this putting-Lily-down-every-chance-we-get."

Lily closed her eyes and waited for the retorts from Joe and Art.

I'm not putting her down. I'm saying it like it is, Art would say.

I am! Joe would pipe up. *It's fun to put her down!*

But nobody said anything. When Lily peeked, Joe was wiggling his foot, and Art was just staring at Mom and looking white around the mouth.

"I've let it go because we've always teased in our house and I thought your brand of kidding was just what boys did. I owe you an apology for this, Lily, but even I thought you needed a little humbling now and then."

"What's 'humbling'?" Joe's face brightened, as if he saw a small chance to save himself.

"Being shown that you aren't perfect," Mom said. "I thought Lily might consider herself to be a cut above the rest of us." She looked at Lily, and her eyes got soft again. "But it appears I was wrong."

"Uh, *yeah*," Art said. "She'd have to be a psycho to think she was perfect after what she pulled last night."

"Would you know what to do about a grease fire?" Mom's knife-voice was back.

"I wouldn't have poured water on it," Art said. "That's why we have a fire extinguisher in the kitchen. Du-uh!"

"Stop," Mom said. "You have never been in that situation, so I doubt you know what you'd do. Your father tried to put the thing out with his hands, for heaven's sake. We just react. It's something we almost can't control. But we can control how we talk to each other. And from here on out, there will be no more teasing that hurts people's feelings." She raised her hand. "I'm just as guilty as anyone else. I'm going to have to work on it. We all will." Nobody said anything. Lily waited to feel like she'd just won a trophy or something. But the feeling didn't come.

I think I deserve to get my feelings hurt, she thought.

And yet, before the rest of that thought could curl through her head, it was as if Kathleen came in and snipped it off with a pair of scissors, leaving only the words, *Father, will You help her to see past her shame and her guilt and to run to You with open arms again?*

❀

She did run to one set of father's arms—Dad's—the minute she got into the hospital room. They were bandaged arms, but he held them out to her, and she ran into the circle they made and started crying all over again.

"Hi, Dad," Art said from the doorway. "Me and Joe

are gonna go look for a Coke machine. We'll come back when she's done doin' that."

"That Art is an old softie," Dad murmured into Lily's hair. "Hates to see a woman cry."

Lily heard her mother give a little snort, and she could feel her father's chest vibrating with his laughter, and all of a sudden she was laughing too. Laughing and crying and snorting and snuffling until a towel had to be produced to wipe off the front of Dad's hospital gown.

"I brought you your own pj's anyway," Mom told him. "I hope you haven't gone waltzing down the hall in that gown. It doesn't close all the way in the back."

"Mo-om!"

"And speaking of waltzing down halls," Mom went on, "we need to talk to you about tomorrow, hon."

Dad was the "hon" she was addressing this time. Lily tried to keep her chin up. She could only do it as long as she kept remembering: *Have God-confidence.*

"Ah, the big modeling show." Dad nodded. "I'm sorry you have to miss that, Lilliputian. Life sure isn't fair sometimes."

"But the doctors see no reason why she shouldn't do it," Mom said. "And Kathleen wants her to."

Dad's eyebrows looked surprised. Lily noticed for the first time that they were a little singed on top. She felt horrible all over again.

God-confidence. God-confidence.

"How do you feel about it?" Dad said to Lily.

Lily waited for Mom to answer for her, but she didn't. Everybody, including, it seemed, the old man in the next bed, was waiting for Lily.

"I'm mixed up," Lily said. "Kathleen says it's not about being beautiful; it's about having God-confidence.

But with you lying here in the bed all bandaged up and everything, I'd feel so, you know, shallow. I mean, it just doesn't seem that important anymore, like Mom's volleyball tournament. She even sent her assistant coach to start a tournament game so she could bring us here."

Dad's eyes darted from one of them to the other, and Lily could almost see a little rubber ball bouncing around in his head. She watched him as he "caught" it. He was much better at collecting his thoughts than he was at finding his glasses.

"I like that term, *God-confidence*," he said. "In fact, that's the first thing I've heard about this whole modeling business that I do like. I think that's the operative phrase here."

"What's an 'operative phrase'?" Lily said. She felt like Joe.

"The one thing that makes it all work," Dad said. With a grunt, he wiggled himself up on the bed. "It takes God-confidence for your mother to go to that volleyball tournament tomorrow and put me out of her head long enough to do the job those girls are depending on her to do."

He shot Mom a look that, as far as Lily could see, meant they'd already had this conversation earlier.

"And," he went on, "it will take God-confidence for you to walk out on that stage with bandages on your face because you've made a commitment and you're honoring it. How much God-confidence would it take for you to skip the show just so you can sit here with me and wallow around in your own guilt?"

"I don't need God to help me do that," Lily said. "I've been doing that all day practically."

"Then I think you have your answer."

It looked as if *that* conversation was over too, until Dad rested his head back on his bed and said, "But the final decision is up to you, Lilliputian. You talk it over with God, and whatever you two decide, your mother and I will respect."

So Lily did what Dad suggested. And this time she didn't put it off until later. While Art and Joe were telling Dad how cool the suite was at the Comfort Inn and were checking out his remote to see if the hospital got any more channels than the hotel did, Lily went down to a little waiting room at the end of the hall that had square furniture and magazines with curled-up corners and a TV that murmured away at nobody. She switched it off, wound herself into a ball on a couch, and closed her eyes. And there it was: a picture of herself running into some very wide-open arms.

God? What do I do? she whispered into them.

If God answered right then, she didn't hear Him. She was asleep within seconds. But when Mom came in and woke her up and led her down the hall to the elevator, she already knew what to do.

"Can you take me to the middle school tomorrow?" she asked as the doors slid closed.

"So, you're doing the show?" Mom asked.

"You're kidding," Art said.

"What are you going to do, wear a bag over your head?" Joe said.

Immediately he clapped both hands over his mouth and bugged his big brown eyes out at Mom.

"Old habits die hard, don't they?" Mom said.

Lily didn't know about that, but she *was* sure about one thing. She was *very* glad she'd never found a way to get Shad Shifferdecker to the show.

Thirteen

The swelling in Lily's forehead had gone down some when she woke up the next morning, but she still felt like a red blowfish as she stumbled into the bathroom for Mom to change the dressings on her cheeks while the boys slept on their fold-out couch.

"We're not supposed to let the burns stay wet," Mom said. "I don't think they're oozing quite as badly as yesterday."

Lily held her breath as Mom carefully pulled the dressing free. What was it going to look like under there? There was a sudden vision of red, twisted flesh writhing on her face like—

But that was only a vision. The reflection in the mirror showed a cheek dotted with flattened blisters, on skin even redder than her forehead.

"A few more seconds over that grease pan and you'd be in the bed next to your dad right now," Mom said. "But this really isn't that bad, is it?"

When Lily didn't shake her head, Mom just dabbed gently at her left cheek with a cool, moist towel and said, "How are we going to get through this day, us two?"

Lily caught her eye in the mirror in surprise. Mom's brown eyes were dewy.

"I'm serious," Mom said. "I usually just plow right through things and never think about how I'm doing it, but I can't do that today. I've got one more game. You have a show. What's your plan? I know you have one."

Lily looked straight into the mirror, as if she were looking into the lens of a video camera. An answer didn't come to her as easily as it did at Rutledge when they were doing slating. She grabbed at the first thing that popped into her head.

"I guess I'm going to pray a lot," Lily said. "Dad says God-confidence is good, and so does Kathleen, so—"

"What does Lily say?"

"I don't know," Lily said. "I don't think it's working yet. But I'm trying."

"Good enough for me," Mom said. "We'll compare notes at the end of the day."

She went to work on the other cheek and then re-bandaged both of them while she told Lily that Mrs. Johnson was going to be at the show with a digital recorder so that she and Dad and Art wouldn't have to totally miss seeing it.

"Art won't want to look at the video," Lily said. "Neither will Joe."

"Joe won't have to. He's going to be there in person."

Lily groaned. "Please don't make him come, Mom. All he'll do is whine about it and give me a hard time."

"I'm not 'making' him. He said he wanted to."

"No, he did not!"

Mom blinked. She wasn't familiar with Reni's little

phrases. "Yeah, he did," she said. "I didn't ask him why, mind you. I didn't want to push it."

"He probably wants to boo me or something."

Mom stopped with the sterile gauze poised in her hand. "Lily, that little speech I made yesterday wasn't just for the boys' benefit. It applies to you too. They're going to find it so much easier to cut you slack if you cut them some too." She put the gauze pad loosely in place. "Besides, though heaven knows I'm not the person you want to come to for beauty tips, I do know this much: nobody looks particularly beautiful when she's hitting somebody between the eyeballs with some evil remark."

Lily's eyes darted to the mirror. Her mouth *didn't* look like the envy of every woman in America at that moment. It was actually curled up and looking hateful.

"I'm sorry," she said. "I love you, Mom."

The next glance at her face showed someone no longer ugly. Just bandaged-up and sad.

Mom dropped her off at the middle school at the appointed time, two hours before the show was supposed to start.

"I'll send Joe over in time," Mom said. "You keep praying. It's working for me already."

"You'll win. You've already won two nights in a row."

"If we do win, I won't see you until late tonight. Mrs. Johnson will take you to her house, and I'll pick you up there."

Lily nodded and started to walk away with her makeup bag, full of brushes, cleanser, and hair clips; but Mom poked her head out the window again.

"Don't forget to check your buns for Cheerios," she

called, eyes twinkling. "And, Lil, I wish I could be here. I really do."

Lily stopped backing away and looked at her. Mom really did seem to be stretched in three directions at once. Lily felt her eyes well up.

"I don't have to do the show," she said. "I can just come to your game—"

"And disappoint God?" Mom said. "No way! You've already talked to Him. It's a done deal. I love you."

"Go in already, before you get picked up for loitering!" Art called out the window. But he had a smile on his face, a big one like Lily's.

Lily smiled back, and she felt an inch more sure—until she got backstage, where everyone stopped brushing their hair and looking for tights to stare at her. Kathleen breezed through them, turning heads back to mirrors with her fingertips and beaming at Lily.

"I knew you'd make the right choice." She squeezed Lily's shoulder. "You're going to be so glad you did this."

"*I* sure wouldn't do it," Lily heard Cassie whisper as she and Kathleen passed by.

"No, you wouldn't," Cassie's mother whispered back. "Because I'd have killed you already for burning yourself in the first place after what we've paid for this course."

I'm sure glad she's not my mother, Lily thought. And then her eyes teared up again as she thought of Mom not being in the audience—of Mom being over at the high school, trying to concentrate on volleyball instead of Dad.

"We have plenty of help for you to make your changes," Kathleen was saying. "Tess will be with you the whole time."

Lily blinked back her tears and tried to concentrate. "What's my number in the lineup now?" she asked.

Kathleen's eyebrows lifted. "Number one."

"I'm still first? But . . . why?"

"Why not? What's changed?"

Lily tried not to look too disgusted. She could already feel her neck going blotchy.

"You have bandages on your face," Kathleen continued. "But you are still the same person you were when I assigned you that number, and I see no reason to change it."

"Let me switch with her." Lily turned to see both Cassie and her mother watching them from three mirrors down. Mama was nudging Cassie forward as if she were holding a cattle prod.

"No," Kathleen said firmly. "There is no need to switch. Nor is there any need for moms back here. Did I neglect to mention that?"

"No, you said it," about three young voices piped up.

Cassie's mother scowled and snatched up her purse. "Something decent-paying better come out of this," Lily heard her mutter as she swept past on her way to the door. "Then I can buy out this whole agency."

If Kathleen heard it, she wasn't showing it. She just ran her beautifully manicured hand down Lily's arm and smiled at her. "God and I have talked," she said quietly. "It's all right. You have the confidence."

Lily swallowed away *all* the tears and nodded. "Okay. Which one's my mirror?"

"The one with all the flowers, I think." Kathleen's eyes were twinkling almost right out of their sockets as she pointed down the row of chairs and mirrors. Lily let out one of her gasps.

On her dressing table were two huge bouquets of flowers with enormous silky bows and actual florist's cards with her name written on them. Lily's hands were shaky as she opened the first one—the one with the yellow ribbon and two dozen happy-faced daisies.

"I am with you in spirit," it said. "Love, Daddy."

Before she even thought about it, Lily put the card to her lips and kissed it. By now, several of the other girls had gathered around, but no one snickered. Their eyes were all wide with envy.

"Open the other one," Stinky said.

"That sure is a *pink* bow," Cassie said.

Lily started to grin. She already knew who this was from, and she was right. "We will all be there cheering for you. Love, the GIRLZ."

"They spelled *girls* wrong," said Cassie from over her shoulder.

"Not *my* Girlz," Lily said. Then she looked at Kathleen. "Will we be able to see the people in the audience with the lights in our eyes?"

"Once in a while you can pick someone out," Kathleen said. "Mostly it's just a sea of faces."

Then I'm glad they sent me this, Lily thought, pressing the card into her palm. *They're coming. They're not ashamed of me at all.*

Then maybe I shouldn't be ashamed of myself *either. Because God isn't.*

She wasn't sure where that thought came from, but it made her feel a little less red and puffed up and oozy looking. And when she was dressed in her "casual" outfit, complete with the cool hat, and looked in the mirror, she was even able to smile.

"Atta girl," Tess said. "But you're not wearing the hat through your whole walk, are you?"

"No," Kathleen said as she was passing by. "The hat comes off when she gets to the end of the runway." She stopped to look into the mirror from behind Lily. "Nothing has changed—remember?"

Lily nodded and took off the hat. She was suddenly one big bandage again. "Anybody need a model to sell sterile gauze?" she said.

"I'm impressed," Tess said, nudging Lily with her elbow. "You still have your sense of humor. I'd be snapping everybody's head off."

Lily shrugged and returned the hat to her head and prayed one more time. *I need confidence, God. Please don't let them stare at me like I'm horrible. And if they do, please don't let me cry until I get back here.*

And then she tried very hard to believe that He would answer. Somehow.

When they started the lineup in the wings and Kathleen was doing her own final hair check before she went out onstage, there was a commotion by the back door. Heads craned that way as Tess waved her arms at Kathleen.

"Wait," Kathleen whispered to the stage manager and then hurried to the door.

"I bet it's Cassie's mother trying to get back in," the girl behind Lily whispered.

"No!" somebody else whispered. "It's Lily's mother!"

Lily's breath caught as she watched Mom follow Kathleen toward her. She could almost smell the sweat on her, and she could see that her hair was sticking out in all directions like she'd been pulling on it for hours.

But Lily was ready to run right into her arms and would have if Mom hadn't held her off, laughing.

"You don't want to touch me," she whispered hoarsely. "I'm disgusting. I just wanted you to know we'd all be in the audience—the boys and me."

"How come?"

"We lost."

"Oh no!"

"Wasn't meant to be. But this was." Mom kissed the tip of her finger and placed it so lightly on Lily's forehead, she could hardly even feel it. "Break a leg, Lil—or whatever it is you models do."

Then she flashed a grin and disappeared, and Kathleen turned Lily to face her.

"Look at that smile," she whispered to Lily. "I mean this sincerely. You have never looked more beautiful."

For some reason, Lily knew she'd never *felt* more beautiful either. Thinking about the Girlz and Mom being out there, and even Art and Joe, all loving her and pulling for her, and Kathleen introducing the class so proudly, even telling about Lily's accident, and God up there just wanting her to have confidence in Him—she didn't let her smile fade. Not even when the music started and she straightened her shoulders and picked her focus point and headed across the stage and down the runway.

Bag slung jauntily over her shoulder, she strolled to the end, got ready to pivot, and then stopped, just the way Kathleen had told her to. Taking a deep breath, she reached up and with a flourish pulled off her hat.

No one in the audience gasped. No one snickered. No one sighed with pity. She only heard her music. Lily executed her perfect pivot with real confidence and turned to the audience on either side of the runway behind her to deliver them all a brilliant smile.

Once in a while you'll be able to pick out a face, Kathleen had said.

And she'd been right. Lily did pick out one, one with shiny braces and beady little eyes.

There, right there at her modeling show, was Shad Shifferdecker himself.

Fourteen

It took a couple of seconds before Shad's eyes met Lily's, and even then it seemed to take a few more for him to register that he was looking at Lily. When he did, the expression on his face wasn't the one Lily had been dreaming about for weeks.

Oh, his mouth fell open, all right, and his beady little eyes blinked in disbelief. But the awestruck eyebrows were missing, and so was the oh-Lily-you're-so-gorgeous-I'll-never-pick-on-you-again look. He simply stared as if he were stunned. Lily knew if she waited much longer for anything else, Kathleen was going to get a cane and pull her offstage.

Making one more clean little pivot, Lily headed back up the runway, hit the stage, and turned for her final smile.

If they've ever been to a fashion show, they'll clap then, Kathleen had told the class in rehearsal.

She hadn't told them that the audience would burst into hurricane-strength applause and holler and whistle and then stand up. But they did.

For a moment, Lily didn't know what to do. Her mind was still spinning from seeing Shad Shifferdecker gaping up at her, and she felt confusion chase the smile right off her lips.

And then her eye caught on two more familiar faces—Joe's and Art's. She caught them in the darkness, just in time to see Joe put his fingers to his lips and execute a whistle that shrilled right up over the rest of the noise. On the other side of Joe, Mom didn't reach over and pop him one. She was too busy clapping and whistling herself.

Lily couldn't have kept another smile off her face if she'd tried. She could almost feel the corners of her mouth meeting in the back of her head, which was just fine, as she plopped her hat back on, rewarded the audience with a wave, and pivoted so briskly her bag gave a merry swing. The audience was still hollering its appreciation when she got to the wings.

"What did I tell you?" Kathleen whispered, eyes sparkling even in the backstage dark.

"That I would be glad I did this," Lily whispered back.

"And?"

"I am!" *And*, she thought suddenly, *I don't even care what Shad Shifferdecker thinks.*

By the time the show was over, Lily was having a hard time getting the smile *off* her face. All the girls were hugging her backstage, and only Cassie looked like she was a little bit jealous. Lily didn't spend any time wondering what Cassie's *mother* was going to have to say about it.

As soon as she walked out the backstage door, Lily was smothered in neck-hugging from all the Girlz and Mrs. Johnson and Mom. Art and Joe drew the line at hugging, but Art did say, "Hey, way to go," and Joe said,

"I didn't even have to use my spitballs." They might as well have told her she was a candidate for Miss America.

The best part came when they bought a pizza and smuggled it into Dad's room at the hospital. Dad had a pretty much nonstop smile himself as Mom popped pepperoni into his mouth and told him all about the show.

"I have never been so proud of her," Mom said. "She was poised and graceful and all that, but it was the *beauty* that came from someplace inside her that really got to me."

"It came from God," Lily said.

There was a momentary disturbance as Art clapped his hand over Joe's mouth, but Dad didn't seem to notice. His face grew soft as he looked at Lily.

"That certainly makes our decision easy, doesn't it?" he said to Mom.

"As far as I'm concerned, it does," Mom said. "And it isn't just that either. Did you know Lily started a support group for girls who get teased at school?"

"Bowwows Anonymous?" The words were out, but Art immediately put up his hands in surrender. "I'm sorry. Lost my head. Won't happen again."

But Lily waved him off and turned to Dad. "Do you mean I can sign on with the agency?"

"Absolutely. Your mom and I have seen a lot of God in what you're doing there. You can keep it up if you want to."

"I can't believe it!" Lily said. She squeezed her eyes shut and let the thrill go through her. She could hear Joe and Art smothering their snickers, but that was really okay.

You can't get to me now, she thought happily. *I'm going to be a professional model!*

All the way home that night she envisioned herself posing in front of the cameras, wearing a smile and clothes from Old Navy. It was a perfect vision, like a reflection in a pool that didn't have a ripple, until Mom dropped a pebble right in the center of it.

She came into the tiny bedroom they were sharing at the Comfort Inn just as Lily was getting ready to slip under the covers and daydream some more until she fell asleep.

"How do you feel?" Mom asked.

"Sensational!"

"I meant your face."

"Oh, I almost forgot all about it!"

"Well, let's not 'forget' to change your bandages tomorrow morning before we go to church." She plopped down onto the bed, then sank back against the pillows with a huge sigh. "You know, it'll probably be a while before Kathleen sends you out on any jobs. It's going to take time for these burns to heal up."

"I can wait." Lily found herself sitting up very tall in the bed. Reni had been right. She did feel like a girl in a book, very brave and heroic.

"That'll give you time to rearrange your schedule too."

"What do you mean?" Lily asked.

That was when Mom dropped the pebble. "Your girls group," she said. "You won't be able to meet with them *every day* if you're going out on jobs."

"But that'll be just, um, once in a while," Lily said.

Mom shook her head. "From what Kathleen told me—and granted, we only spoke briefly—but she said once you're completely well, she plans to keep you very busy. I didn't realize it, but she has contacts in New York,

Chicago even. One woman who was at the show tonight from *Boston* asked Kathleen specifically about you."

"No, she did not!"

"What is that expression anyway? Whatever happened to 'Shut *up*'?"

Lily felt her stomach turning over. "So I'm going to be going out to auditions, like, all the time?"

"I told her not during school hours, and she agreed. But it does mean right *after* school in most cases. These folks like to get their work done during the business day. Luckily, Dad's schedule is such that once *he's* back in the driver's seat, he'll be able to drive you."

Mom gave her dry little non-smile. "Right now, of course, you two are a real pair. I bet I've dealt with a mile of sterile gauze in the last two days . . ."

But Lily didn't hear the rest. Her mind was squealing to a stop and leaving long tire treads in her head.

I can't go to all *the Girlz Only meetings?* she thought. *But what about Zooey and Suzy? They're just getting started on their God-confidence. And Reni—she's my best friend—I can't just dump her to go do whatever. And what about . . .*

What about me?

Suddenly the thought of being in New York with a bunch of people who might not be as nice as Kathleen, who might be like—like Cassie's mother or something—suddenly that was the loneliest thing she could think of.

Have God-confidence, she told herself sternly.

Lily looked over at her mother, who had drifted off to sleep in midsentence. Lily pulled the covers up over her and snapped out the light. Then she lay there in the darkness, trying to get the ripples out of her perfect vision. But God-confidence didn't make them disappear.

By Monday morning, it seemed like everybody from the school custodian to Ashley Adamson had heard some version of all the things that had happened to Lily since last Thursday.

"I heard you burned your whole house down and now you're gonna be on *Dateline*," Marcie said before Lily could even get her backpack off.

"Somebody told me there was a fire during some fashion show you were in," Leo said.

"Maybe we ought to have a lesson about rumors today," Ms. Gooch said. "How's your father, Lily?"

"Was he in the fashion show too?" Daniel said.

One person who didn't add anything to the discussion was Shad Shifferdecker, and for almost the first time since Saturday, Lily focused her attention on him.

He was sitting in his usual spot, one row over from Lily, and he was slouched down in typical Shad fashion, one shoulder higher than the other, one foot hooked into the book rack under the desk. But, not at all like usual, he was paying absolutely no attention to the conversation going on around him. He was rolling a pencil up and down on the desktop, watching it as if it were hypnotizing him.

Huh, Lily thought. *Maybe I did impress him after all.*

No. Maybe God impressed him. Maybe my prayers are being answered, and he isn't going to tease me anymore now that he's seen me onstage.

Just then Shad looked up, and his eyes hooked onto Lily's. They narrowed.

"What are you lookin' at, freak?" he asked. "Dude, it creeps me out when you stare at me like that!"

But the only thing Lily was thinking at that moment

was that she wasn't gritting her teeth. Not even a little bit.

That was so encouraging that at first break she asked Reni and Suzy and Zooey to wait for her by the tree. Then she went right up to Shad at the water fountain and said, "So how come you came to my modeling show after all?"

He turned around, mouth still dripping, and wiped his lips on his shirtsleeve. "It wasn't *my* idea, I'll tell ya that."

"You didn't go to the mall?" Lily said.

"I guess not if I was at your stupid thing. Duh!"

"But I thought you always went to the mall on Saturday."

"So I didn't go last Saturday. Sue me!"

Lily shrugged. So far, nothing had changed with Shad Shifferdecker. He was just as obnoxious as ever.

"Are you done interrogatin' me?" he said.

Lily was about to say no, that she had a few more questions, when out of the corner of her eye she caught sight of Reni and Zooey waving frantically to her.

"I have to go," she told Shad.

"Like I care."

Lily tossed her hair and took off at a brisk walk for the tree.

"Thanks for giving me an excuse to come over here," she said to the Girlz. "He's just as hateful as he ever was—"

"We found out why Shad was at the show!" Zooey said. Her little round face was flushed pink, and she was squeezing the life out of Suzy's arm.

"You did? How?" Lily asked.

They both looked at Suzy, who gave the expected nervous giggle.

"Suzy's mama works at the high school," Reni said.

"She's a secretary over there," Zooey put in.

"She heard Mrs. Shifferdecker talking because Mrs. Shifferdecker *teaches* at the high school."

"And guess what?" Zooey asked. Lily was sure she was about to explode like a bobbing pink balloon.

"What?"

"Shad doesn't *ever* hang out at the mall on Saturday. His mother drags him wherever she goes! If she comes up to the school to work in her classroom, she makes him come with her so he won't get in any trouble!"

Zooey had to stop for breath, and Reni dove in. "Saturday she must have been working at the school and stuck him in the auditorium to watch whatever was going on to get him out of her hair."

For a minute, all Lily could do was stare at them. She waited for the big bubble of triumphant laughter to fly out of her throat, or at least the string of "I knew Shad Shifferdecker was a liar!"

But all she found herself doing was looking at Suzy.

"Did you tell Reni and Zooey all that?" Lily asked her.

Suzy nodded.

"It was the most I ever heard her say all at one time," Zooey put in.

"All at one time?" Reni raised her hands. "It's the most I ever heard her say *period*. The whole time I've known her."

"Wow." Lily *did* feel a bubble in her chest, but it felt good, like how being proud feels. She smiled. "You're getting confidence, Suzy."

"I am?" Suzy smiled too. And then, of course, she giggled.

"But we have to get rid of the giggle at the end of every sentence," Lily said. "We can work on that."

"Can we have a meeting today?" Zooey asked. "I miss them."

"We can have a meeting today," Lily said. And to herself she said, "And maybe every day." She still wasn't sure about this modeling thing. She was going to have to talk to God about it some more.

Just then the bell rang, and the Girlz linked arms to head for the building.

"Let's all try to walk the exact same way," Lily started to say.

But she was interrupted by a scream that split through the schoolyard noise like a chain saw. All four of them had to stop short to keep from being plowed into by a tousle-headed figure holding the back of her head.

"That's Kresha!" Zooey said as the girl flew past.

"What happened?" Reni said.

It didn't take a rocket scientist to figure it out. Lily started to scan the schoolyard with her eyes and spotted three boys folded in half and clutching at their sides as if they were in pain, though their faces were all twisted with laughter.

"I mighta known it was Shad and them," Reni exploded. "What have they done to their hair?"

The four girls looked curiously as Shad, Leo, and Daniel straightened up. Lily let out a disgusted puff of air. All three of them had their hair completely messed up and sticking out, the way Kresha's always was. Leo was holding a brush, and Daniel had a can of mousse.

"Those evil boys tried to trade hairdos with her." Lily narrowed her eyes. "I'd bet a hundred dollars."

"I'd bet a thousand," Zooey said. Her face was the color of a strawberry.

"They're evil," Suzy said. Her face turned suddenly so fierce that Lily wanted to laugh. But instead she folded her arms and tossed back her hair. "Kresha needs to be in the Girlz Only Group. Anybody have any objections?"

"She needs to be," Reni said. "First thing *we* need to do is help her find a different 'do so they can't tease her about it anymore."

Lily shook her head. "They'd still tease her. And they're still gonna tease us, no matter what we do."

Zooey now looked like a *confused* strawberry.

"Then what's the point of the club?" Reni said. "I thought we were trying to make it so Shad would never have any reason to tease us."

"I don't think that anymore," Lily said. "I think we just need to have so much confidence that it doesn't *bother* us anymore when he teases us."

Zooey rolled her eyes. "You're talking about self-confidence. My mama talks about that all the time. She says I don't have any."

"No," Lily said. "I'm talking God-confidence."

"Are you girls joining us in class?" Ms. Gooch called to them from across the schoolyard. "Or should I have your desks brought out here?"

They broke into a run, Suzy zipping out in front, Zooey trailing behind. Lily linked her arm through Reni's.

"Let's ask Kresha to sit with us at lunch and invite her into the group," Lily said as they ran.

"Okay." Reni paused. "Lily, what's *God*-confidence?"

Lily tilted her head to think. "It's how I walked right up to Shad Shifferdecker today and asked him how come he was at the middle school Saturday and not the mall."

"No, you did not!"

"And when he was hateful to me, it didn't cut me in half like it used to."

"Girl, that was brave."

"Nope," Lily said again. "That was God."

"I never heard *that* at church."

"I didn't learn it at church." Lily let her smile meet in the back. "I learned *that* at modeling school."

Check out this excerpt from the next book in the Lily Series!

Lily Robbins, MD (Medical Dabbler)

Psst! Snobbins!" Lily Robbins didn't have to look up from the pizza boxes she was carrying to know that voice. It was Shad Shifferdecker—the most obnoxious kid in the entire sixth grade. She tossed her mane of red hair and, as usual, ignored him.

And, as usual, he persisted. That was one of the things that made him so obnoxious.

"Snobbins!" he hissed again. "Are you gonna eat all that pizza yourself? Dude!"

Lily just kept moving toward the door out of Papa John's. *Just a couple more steps and I'll be away from the absurd little creep*, she told herself. *And the sooner the better.*

She leaned against the glass door and pushed herself out into the freezing January air.

"See ya tomorrow," Shad said behind her. "If you can get through the classroom door—"

The door slapped shut, and Lily hurried toward the maroon van where her mom was waiting with the motor running and the heater blasting. But even though Lily couldn't hear him anymore, she knew Shad wasn't finished with her. He never was.

Don't look back, she warned herself. *Or you'll see something gross.*

Still, just as she reached the van, she caught a glimpse of her mom's face. It was twisted up into a question mark as she stared inside Papa John's. Lily couldn't help it. She took a glance over her shoulder—and immediately wished she hadn't.

There was Shad at the door, his whole jacket crammed inside his T-shirt and his cheeks puffed out to three times their normal size so that he looked like a demented version of the Pillsbury Doughboy.

"You are *so* not funny!" Lily wanted to shout at him.

Instead she flipped her head around and stomped toward the van. Or, at least she *tried* to. On her second step, her heel slid on the ice, and she careened crazily forward, juggling pizza boxes and heading for a collision with the frozen ground.

The pizzas hit first, with Lily right on top of them. She could feel the warmth of the grease through the box against her cheek. The smell of pepperoni went right up her nose.

Above her she could hear the van window on the passenger side going down.

"You all right, Lil?" Mom said.

"Yeah," Lily answered through her teeth.

"Is the pizza all right?"

Lily moaned and peeled herself off the pile of slightly flattened boxes. "I bet all the topping is stuck to the cardboard now," she said.

"Don't worry about it," Mom said. "Just get in the van before you freeze your buns off—and our dinner gets cold."

Lily did, although she wasn't as worried about her buns or the pizza as she was about the story Shad Shifferdecker was going to spread to their whole class tomorrow. But she didn't even risk a glance inside Papa John's as she climbed into the van and examined the top pizza.

"I think it's okay," she said while Mom was backing out of the parking place and mercifully leaving Shad behind. "Just some pepperoni stuck to the lid, but I can peel that off."

"And I would if I were you," Mom said dryly, "before your brothers get a look at it and want to know what happened."

"Mom, please don't—"

"How much is it worth to you for me to keep my mouth shut?"

Mom's mouth was twitching the way it always did when she was teasing. She never smiled that much, although the twinkle in her big, brown doe-eyes usually gave her away.

"You're not gonna tell," Lily said.

"Who was that delightful child in the pizza place?" Mom said, lips still twitching. "Friend of yours?"

"No, he is NOT! Gross me out and make me icky!"

"Come on now, Lil. Don't hold back. Tell me how you really feel."

"I can't stand Shad Shifferdecker," Lily said, inspecting pizza number two. "He *cannot* leave me alone. He's in my face all the time, telling me my hair looks like it's on fire, or my mouth looks like I got stung by something big, or my skin's so white it blinds him when I'm out in the sun."

"Charming," Mom said. "How's the one with the works? Art will go ballistic if his sausage is mixed up with his Canadian bacon."

Lily pried open the lid to the pizza on the bottom and wrinkled her nose. "How do you know whether it's messed up or not?" she said. "It always looks like somebody already ate it to me, with all that stuff on there."

"Lily, hold on!"

Mom's arm came out and flattened against Lily's chest. The van swerved sharply and suddenly felt as if it were out of control. Lily looked up just in time to see a pair of taillights in front of them disappear as the car spun around. Headlights glared in their faces.

"Mom!" Lily screamed.

She squeezed her eyes shut and, for some reason she couldn't figure out, clutched the pizza boxes against her.

She felt the van lurch to a stop, and she waited for the crash that was surely going to kill them both. But all she heard was her mother's gasp.

"Oh, dear Lord!"

Lily opened her eyes again. The other car had spun once more and was sailing across the road, straight toward a pickup truck coming from the other direction. As Lily and her mother watched, the two vehicles slammed together and crumpled like . . . like two pizza boxes. Metal smashed. Glass broke. And then it was as quiet as snow itself.

"Dear Lord," Mom said again. Only this time her voice was quiet and grim as she reached for the cell phone and punched in three numbers.

"Do you think anybody got hurt?" Lily said.

She knew the answer was obvious, but it was the only thing that came into her head.

"There's been an accident on Route 130," Mom was saying into the phone.

How could somebody not get hurt in that? Lily thought. She shuddered and tried not to think of what the people inside must look like.

Mom hung up the phone and grabbed her gloves. "I'm going to go see if I can do anything before the paramedics get here."

"You're going *over* there?" Lily said.

"I'd want somebody to come help us if we'd been the ones that got hit." Mom pulled her knit cap down over her ponytail. "And we almost were."

A chill went through Lily, and it wasn't from the blast of frosty air that came in as her mother opened the van door. *It could have been us, all crumpled up and maybe bleeding—*

It wasn't a thought she wanted to be left alone with. She got out of the van and followed her mother, picking her way across the ice.

"Lil, why don't you stay here until I know what's happened," Mom said.

"I want to come," Lily said. Her own voice sounded thin and scared.

"Then get some blankets out of the back, and the first-aid kit."

Lily didn't even know there *was* a first-aid kit in the van. It didn't strike her as a Mom kind of thing. Whenever Lily or her younger brother, Joe, or her older brother, Art, got hurt, Mom would say, "Are you hemorrhaging? Have a bone sticking out?" When the answer was no, she'd tell them to go get a Band-Aid and not whine about it.

But there *was* a first-aid kit in the back of the van, along with two blankets and even a pillow. Lily grabbed all of it and made her way over to the side of the road.

Mom was there with some other people who had stopped, and they were all crouched around somebody on the ground. As soon as Lily got close, Mom put her hand up and said, "That's far enough, Lil. Just leave the stuff here."

There was no merry twitching around her mother's mouth now. Her tan face was white, and her voice was strained. Lily backed away, heart pounding.

"Could we have one of those blankets over here?" someone said.

Lily looked up. There was a teenage boy, around Art's age, crouched down beside a small person. The child was sitting up. It was probably safe to go over there. Lily grabbed one of the blankets she'd just set down and slipped and slid across the ice to get to them.

"I don't think he's hurt," the teenager said to Lily, "but he's shaking like he's freezing."

Lily squatted beside him. A boy of about five blinked up at Lily out of a face the color of cream of wheat. His lips were blue, and the teenager was right: he was trembling like a leaf about to fall off a tree.

"You want a blanket?" Lily said to him.

He didn't answer, but Lily wrapped it around him anyway and then rubbed her hands up and down his arms, the way her dad did to her when she was whining about being in danger of frostbite if she had to walk to school.

"I don't think he's hurt," the teenager said again. "He's probably not, huh?"

Lily looked up at him in surprise. He was shaking as badly as the little boy was, and even in the dark Lily could see tears shimmering in his eyes.

"He doesn't look like he is," Lily said.

"Nah, I bet he's not."

The teen crossed his arms over his chest and stuck his hands into his armpits. His bottom lip was vibrating.

"Did you ask him?" Lily said.

"He won't say nothin'. He just sits there. But he's probably not hurt."

The teenager just kept shaking his head. Lily got a strange feeling, like the kid didn't really know what he was saying. Mouth suddenly dry, Lily turned to the little boy.

"What's your name?" she said.

The little blue lips came open. "Thomas," he said in a voice she could hardly hear.

"I'm Lily," she said.

"Lily," he said.

The teenager let out a shrill laugh. "You see! He's not hurt, huh?"

"Do you have any *owies*, Thomas?" Lily said.

"What's an 'owie'?" the teenage boy said.

But before Lily had a chance to say, "You know, a boo-boo, a cut or a scrape or something," the air was filled with the screaming of sirens. The teenager's face drained, and his eyes went wild.

"I just lost control!" he said. "It was the ice! I couldn't help it!"

His voice was so frightened that even little Thomas started to cry. Lily put her hands on his arms to rub them again, but he stuck his own arms out and hurled himself against her. There was nothing to do but fold him up in a hug.

"It's okay, Thomas," Lily said to him. "You're okay."

The teenage boy was *not* okay. The minute a police officer got out of his car and started toward him, the kid broke into tears. It made Lily feel like she wanted to be somewhere else. Fortunately, the policeman took him aside.

But then little Thomas started to whimper.

"You're okay," Lily said. "You aren't hurt. It's okay—"

"I am too hurt," Thomas said.

Lily pulled him away from her a little and looked at him. "Where?" she said.

"My tummy," he said. "It hurts a lot."

"Oh," Lily said.

She looked around for someone to call to, but the flock of uniformed adults who had just arrived all seemed to be either running around or hovering around the person on the ground. Lily looked back at Thomas. He was leaning over at the middle now, and his eyes were looking funny, like he couldn't quite focus them.

"Um . . . why don't you lie down, and I'll get somebody to help us," Lily said.

"Don't leave!" Thomas said, and he clutched at her sleeve with his fingers. Lily noticed for the first time that he didn't have gloves on, and his little fingers were red and stiff.

"Okay, but lie down. And put these on."

She peeled off her knit mittens and slid them over his tiny hands. Then she got him to curl up in the blanket with his head in her lap.

"You smell like pizza," he murmured.

It was the kind of voice a person used when he was

about to fall asleep, and it scared Lily. She twisted around and caught sight of a paramedic walking away from the person on the ground, right toward them.

"This one's okay?" the paramedic called to her.

"I don't think so," Lily called back. "He says his stomach hurts. And his eyes look funny and his lips are blue and he's falling asleep."

The paramedic's steps got faster, and he already had his little flashlight out when he got to them.

"Hey, fella," he said to Thomas as he shined the light in his eyes.

"His name's Thomas," Lily said.

"Stretcher over here!" the paramedic called out. "We're gonna have to take you to the hospital, Thomas," he said.

"Mommy!" Thomas said.

"Mommy's going too, only she's getting a different ride. You'll see her when you get there."

"You come with me."

Thomas was looking right at Lily, his eyes trying hard to stay focused.

"Is this your sister?" the paramedic said.

"I didn't even know him until just now," Lily said.

The paramedic gave a grim grin. "He sure likes you." He went on doing things to Thomas as he talked. "Thanks for staying here with him. The other driver told us he thought the little guy was all right." He grunted softly. "'Course, he has a reason to want him to be all right."

Thomas whimpered, and Lily leaned down over him. "You *will* be okay, Thomas," she said.

"Sure, he will. All right, fella. We're gonna put you on this stretcher and give you a wild ride. How would you like that?"

Thomas's face puckered weakly. "I want *her* to take me."